CAULDRON OF VIOLENCE

Young Colin Bowman, orphaned after an Indian attack, is left homeless and alone. But the Civil War beckons and Colin, fighting for the victorious Union army, finds adventure learning the art of war. After the conflict, Colin's adventures continue, guiding Sam Curtway and his daughter Julia's train safely through Indian country. Colin learns the value of love, and when Indians attack, lives hang in the balance. Now he must settle old scores and move on to a new life.

E. C. TUBB

CAULDRON OF VIOLENCE

Complete and Unabridged

LINFORD
Leicester

First published in Great Britain in 2000

First Linford Edition
published 2010

Originally published in paperback as
Wagon Trail by Charles S. Graham

British Library CIP Data

Tubb, E. C.
   Cauldron of violence. - -
   (Linford western library)
   1. Western stories.
   2. Large type books.
   I. Title II. Series
   823.9′14–dc22

ISBN 978–1–44480–131–6

Published by
F. A. Thorpe (Publishing)
Anstey, Leicestershire

Set by Words & Graphics Ltd.
Anstey, Leicestershire
Printed and bound in Great Britain by
T. J. International Ltd., Padstow, Cornwall

This book is printed on acid-free paper

1

Colin was twelve when his folks died. Uncle Zeke had visited, dropping in at sunset riding a travel-stained mule and yelling as he approached the homestead that he was fit to eat a horse. Colin liked his uncle though he had rarely seen the big, bearded old prospector who roamed the hills in his eternal search for gold. One day, maybe, he would finally strike it rich and then all his grandiose promises would come true.

He was big in his promises, was Uncle Zeke, and, when he had drunk a little too much of the home-brewed whiskey Pa kept by, inclined to forget himself. Like the time when he'd kissed Ma. He'd been friendly enough about it and Colin guessed that he'd meant no harm but Pa had taken it badly and it was only the woman's quick tact which

1

had stopped an argument. But about his promises there could be no argument.

'We'll all head east,' he used to say. 'To New York or down to New Orleans. We'll buy some fancy clothes and a fancy house. Matilda'd like that, wouldn't you girl? And Colin here could go to school.'

Then he'd stretch himself in the hickory chair, his booted feet thrust towards the fire which hissed in protest each time he spat a brown stream of tobacco juice into the red wood ash mounted by blazing logs. Pa would smile and nod, his eyes distant as if already feeling broadcloth on his back instead of homespun and even Ma would sigh at the thought of things she'd never known. Then she'd smile and take up some mending, her thin, work-worn hands almost transparent in the dancing light of the fire as she spliced her needle mending Uncle Zeke's ripped shirts and holed socks that he invariably brought with him.

Colin used to sit up as late as allowed and, even when sent to bed, would hug his knees in the other room and listen to the men talk of old times. He learned a lot that way, more perhaps than anyone guessed. He learned that Uncle Zeke, despite his beard and air of age, wasn't really so old. He was only a few years older than Pa and both had, at one time, courted the same girl. Pa had won and Zeke had taken to prospecting. Which maybe accounted for Pa not liking that kiss that time. Colin didn't know about that, but he did know that all the talk of going east with him and being sent to school upset him. Privately he made a wish that Uncle Zeke wouldn't strike it rich, not if it meant losing his freedom for book learning.

So it usually was when Uncle Zeke came riding in from the hills with his old mule and his heap of mending, his prodigious appetite and his fulsome promises. But this time was different.

Ma had set a plate of belly pork and

beans before the prospector and he forked it into his mouth as if he hadn't eaten for a week. He paused only to tear off hunks of corn bread or take a gulp at the black, scalding coffee sweetened with wild honey. Finally, when Colin thought that he must surely burst if he ate another mouthful, Zeke pushed away his plate and cut himself a chew of tobacco. He used his hunting knife for the job, the razor sharp blade coming to rest on the ball of his calloused thumb. He saw Colin looking at him and winked.

'Want a plug?'

'No thanks.' Colin knew that his uncle was joshing him. Pa laughed.

'Give him another couple of years, Zeke, and he'll be ready for it.' Fondly he ruffled his son's hair. 'Mule bedded down, Colin?'

'I took care of it.'

'You took care of Melly good?' Zeke pointed with his knife. 'I sure value that mule, son, and I'd take it unkindly if you skipped the job.'

'I didn't skip it,' said Colin, and felt the blood rise to his face. 'I can handle stock.'

'Sure he can.' Pa laughed again. 'He does a man's work on the homestead, Zeke. You don't have to worry.'

'One thing,' said Colin, then paused. He was a boy, not a man, and had to remember that. He gained comfort from the prospector's grin.

'What is it?'

'There's a cut on the mule,' said Colin quickly. 'Just back of the saddle. I cleaned it but I thought you'd like to know.'

'I know.' Zeke chewed thoughtfully at his cud. 'Ever seen an arrow wound before, boy?'

'Is that what it is?'

'That's right. A bunch of Indians took a few shots at me while I was riding through Dead Man's Canyon. They was a longs way off but managed to stick Melly.' He spat thoughtfully into the fire. 'That was three days ago.'

'Indians!' Ma turned a little pale and

her eyes looked huge against her face. 'Trouble, Zeke?'

'Maybe, maybe not.' The prospector shrugged. 'Could have been a bunch of young braves out after some easy hair. Or maybe it was a party some trader had fed with whiskey who were feeling their oats. No call to get concerned, Matilda. I told you that it happened three days' ride away.'

'Not so far,' pointed out Pa. He filled and lit his pipe. 'Recognize them?'

'Sioux for my money. Some of Thunder Cloud's braves from their paint.' Zeke shrugged as if the matter were of no importance, which, to him, it wasn't. The West was wild country, a place where a man carried his own law and his own safety in the weapons he bore. Roving bands of Indians were liable to be met at any time and usually the meeting ended with a few shots being fired. Shots from the white man, that is; the Indians used the bone and sinew bows they had carried from the time of the Conquistadors. But usually the Indians concentrated on theft rather than scalps. They envied the white man his horses and mules, his rifles and iron utensils, a craving which they satisfied either through outright attack and theft or by trading furs and robes with the occasional traders who penetrated into the Indian Territory.

Zeke eased himself in his chair and shifted his plug from one cheek to the other.

'Fine place you're making here, John,' he said to his brother. 'Wouldn't recognize it now that you've dug a well and got some crops down. Remember when we stopped?'

'I remember.' John Bowman ran work-calloused fingers through his thinning hair. 'Lucky we did as things turned out. George Donner didn't do so good taking that cut-off.'

'Half the party dead,' said Zeke somberly. 'We could have been with them if Matilda hadn't been near her time.' He chuckled. 'Nothing like a child coming to make a woman forget the California Fever.' He became serious again. 'Seems kinda like fate if you know what I mean. There we were, all three of us with a brand new wagon and all set to reach California. I reckon we'd have done it too. But Matilda had Colin and she looked mighty sickly to ride the wagon. So we pulled out, sold the wagon and traded for farming tools and gear.' He squinted up at the ceiling. 'How long, John? A year, two years afore we had this cabin built?'

'A year,' said Matilda. 'We lived in a tent for the first year.' She shivered at bitter memory. 'I never want to go through another winter like that one again.'

'Worse for the Donners,' reminded Zeke. 'They got trapped in that pass and were snowed in. Forty dead out of eighty odd. I heard tell that they were eating their own dead time rescue came.'

'Let's forget it,' said Matilda firmly. 'That was way back in 1846, over twelve years ago now.' She smiled at her only son. 'Colin will be thirteen come Fall.'

'Seems like yesterday.' Zeke couldn't seem to forget the past. 'There was George Donner and his wife Tamsen. And Reed, you remember him, John? Big red faced feller, always losing his temper. Remember that big wagon he had?'

'The double decker?' John nodded. 'I remember.'

'And Keseburg, a queer one that, and Graves and Stansen and Paddy Doolan.' Zeke sighed. 'Wonder where they all are now?'

'Dead, most of them.' John dragged at his pipe. 'We're lucky not to be with them.'

'We'd have made it,' said Zeke positively. 'I reckon we'd have made it.' He fell silent, staring into the fire. 'Never did see California after all,' he murmured. 'Corn eight feet high, apples as big as melons, just throw down seed and stand back and watch her grow. Remember the tales, John?'

'I remember.'

'I remember other things,' said Matilda sharply. 'I remember the Donners all dead in the snows and their children orphaned. I remember the way the Indians shot our oxen and stole our things. I reckon that we're a sight better off where we are. It's good land and it's ours.' She banged the dishes as she cleared the table. 'Next thing will be that you'll want to build a wagon and set off for California again.'

'Might be an idea at that,' said Zeke, then fell silent at John's frown.

'We ain't moving,' he assured his wife. 'I done promised you that when Colin was born and I don't go back on my word. This is our land and here we stay.' He grinned. 'Unless Zeke strikes it rich, of course, then we head east and get the fancy clothes you've a hankering for.'

'It ain't clothes I'm wanting,' Matilda said sharply. 'It's a school for Colin.' Her eyes softened as she stared at the boy, sitting quiet and watchful by the chimney corner. 'It ain't right that he should grow up in the wilds this way. What's going to become of him?'

'He'll be a man,' said John Bowman. He was fiercely proud of his only child. 'He can read and write and can handle stock. He can hunt too and hit his mark at a hundred paces with a rifle or pistol.'

'So he can read and shoot,' said Matilda scornfully. 'And he can handle stock and farm. But what else? You want your son to grow up an ignorant sod-breaker?'

'Ain't nothing wrong in that.'

'It ain't good enough for Colin,' she said firmly, and made more noise than was necessary as she took the dishes outside to wash them. Zeke raised his eyebrows at his brother and moved his chair nearer to the fire.

'She's upset,' said John. 'Think nothing of it.'

He trimmed and lit a smoking animal-fat lamp; the light, poor though it was, was still luxury to a family that normally rose and bedded with the sun. From a small cupboard he took a stone jug, unstoppered it, took a swig and passed it to Zeke. The prospector slipped his fingers through the handle and, with a practised motion, rested the jug on his forearm, tilting it so as to shoot a generous stream of the raw spirit into his mouth, Matilda returned from her chores as he set it down.

'So you can shoot, can you?' He stared at Colin. 'That your rifle?' He gestured to where an old-fashioned squirrel gun hung on pegs over the fireplace. Below it rested a more modern arm and a powder horn and bullet pouch hung to one side. Next to the bullet pouch, hanging by the trigger guards, hung a couple of pistols.

'Pa says I can.'

'Modest, ain't you?' Zeke burped and grinned. 'No harm in that.' He rose and took down the weapons, hefting them with the ease of a man accustomed to guns. He snapped the old-fashioned flint locks, poised the rifles to his shoulder and replaced them on the pegs. The pistols, again flint locks, he scorned. 'When are you going to buy some decent guns, John?'

'Nothing wrong with those pieces.' John was defensive.

'Thirty years ago, no. Twenty even, but hell, man, they belong to the Ark. Ain't you never heard of percussion caps?'

'Where are we going to get caps out here?' John took a swig of the whiskey. 'I can cut a flint and make my own powder if I have to, bullets too. Why should I spend good money on fancy weapons when they will do just as good?'

'Man, don't you value your life?' Zeke was genuinely disturbed. 'I knew you had these things but figured that you'd change them the first chance you got. You mean to tell me a trader ain't been this way since I called in last?'

'Might have done.' John was casual.

'I give up.' Zeke showed his disgust by gulping at the jug. 'All right, so you're saving your money for the boy, but guns are important, John, you know that.' He wiped his bearded lips. 'What if the Indians come howling down these parts after hair?'

'Ain't seen an Indian for over a month.' John didn't look at his wife. 'The last bunch that called we treated friendly. We get along fine with the Indians.'

'Sure,' said Zeke scornfully. 'So did Melly but she's carrying the mark of a Sioux arrow.' He blew through his nose. 'Mind if I give Colin a present?'

Without waiting for an answer he rose and stepped over to where he had left his pack and saddle. He returned carrying an oddly shaped rifle.

'This is an over and under,' he explained to the wide-eyed boy. 'See, there's a shotgun barrel on the top and a rifled barrel below. The shotgun takes nine buckshot to the load and the rifle takes a twenty to the pound ball. Maybe she's a mite light but I figured it heavy enough for most things.' The weak light

14

of the lamp gleamed off the barrels. 'See, this is a percussion cap model. You load her down the muzzle the same as before but instead of messing about with priming you crimp one of these little copper caps over the nipple.' He demonstrated to the attentive boy, his blunt fingers surprisingly deft as they crimped the little copper envelopes over the nipples of the two barrels.

'Now she ain't loaded,' said Zeke. 'Watch.' He cocked back the hammers, rested his finger on the twin triggers, let it slip to the rear one and pressed. The cap on the shotgun nipple exploded with a sharp report. 'Back trigger for shotgun,' the prospector explained. 'Front for rifle.' He snapped the remaining hammer. 'Fires every time and fires fast. No chance of spilt priming, damp powder or a dull flint. Here.' He held out the weapon.

'For me?' Colin was incredulous.

'For you, and caps to go with it.' Zeke looked disgusted. 'Don't you want it?'

'Want it!' Colin almost snatched the weapon. 'Thanks.'

'Colin!' John was sharp but Zeke shook his head.

'Let the boy be, John, ain't you ever been young?' His eyes softened as he stared at the boy and from him to his brother's wife. The better man had won, he supposed, then dismissed the thought as John passed the jug. Colin, almost unnoticed, sat nursing and examining his gift.

'Heard any news from the east, John?' Tobacco juice hissed as it landed in the fire. 'Kinda got out of touch with things lately. Did Abe Lincoln make the presidency?'

'Not yet he hasn't.' John sucked at his pipe. He felt warm and comfortable with his wife and son beside him and his only brother under his roof. The night had grown darker around the cabin so that no trace of light came through the single window set beside the door. The lamp smouldered and joined with the fire to throw bright

16

shadows over the rough logs which he had cut and erected with his own hands. From the stable came a stirring as of restless mules and he tensed, then dismissed the noise. Naturally the two mules he owned would be restless with a stranger among them.

'He'll make it,' said Zeke. 'I met him once, back in Springfield it was when he was first elected to Congress. Must have been about the time the Donner party set off.' He clucked his tongue. 'Makes a man feel old thinking about the past.'

'You ain't old,' said Matilda. 'But old enough to take a wife and settle down.' Hope gleamed in her eyes. 'Why not Zeke? You could take the next section to ours. There's good water and good land and John would help you as much as he could.'

'Hungry for neighbours, Matilda?' Zeke shook his head. 'Can't say that I blame you, though I've never felt the need for them myself. But don't figure on me. I don't aim to get hog-tied and staked down yet awhile. Not while there's gold in the hills just waiting to fill a man's poke.'

'And Indians waiting to kill him,' she said sharply.

'And Indians,' admitted the prospector. He changed the subject. 'Still, I don't reckon you'll be lonely for long. From what I hear there's more wagon trains heading west from Independence and maybe some of them will stop and settle here.'

'Not if they've got California Fever,' said John sombrely. 'There's no stopping a man once he gets that.'

'You stopped,' reminded Zeke.

'Yes, so I did.' John didn't look at his wife. 'So I did.'

'Have you another drink,' said Zeke and reached for the jug. 'You could be a lot worse than you are, John. You've good land, a good wife and a fine boy. You've got health and you're your own boss. Hell, ain't you ever satisfied?'

The sudden violence in his voice surprised even himself and to cover his emotion he gulped at the jug. Inwardly he cursed himself. A man shouldn't remember the past, the woman he'd lost or the son he didn't have. More, he shouldn't ever come back to see them. He swallowed, the raw spirit burning his throat and stomach, then swallowed again to dull the pain of an old hurt. When he set down the jug his eyes were streaming and he dabbed at them with the back of his hand.

'What you make this from, John, blasting powder?'

'Corn.' John took a swig himself. He was lifting the jug a second time when a sudden, sharp, double explosion almost made him leap from his chair. Colin, looking a little abashed, held his gift in his hands.

'Sorry, Pa,' he said. 'But I was testing the trigger pull and . . . '

'And the caps went off.' Zeke grinned. 'Take them off before testing, son, and then even if it's loaded no one will get hurt.'

John grunted, half pleased, half

annoyed at the boy. Matilda, suddenly reminded of his presence, rose to her feet.

'Bed.'

'But Ma . . . '

'You heard what I said.' She snatched the weapon from him and thrust him towards the door. 'You go and wash now and mind you wash clean.'

'Can I take the gun with me, Ma?'

'Certainly not!'

'Please Ma.' Colin looked pleadingly at her. 'Just to set beside me.'

For a moment she remained firm, then, perhaps because of the memory when she herself had been young and had taken her new work basket to bed with her so that she could see it in the first dawn light, she relented.

'After you wash — and wash good, mind, or the gun stays here.'

Colin's smile warmed her heart as he dived into the night.

2

It was warm in bed under the corn-husk coverlet and between the blankets but Colin couldn't sleep. He lay awake, listening to the soft sough of the wind about the cabin and the thin, distant cries of coyotes as they howled at the moon. From the other room the voices of Uncle Zeke and Pa rose and fell as they attended to the jug, and Ma, in her softer voice, chimed in eager for gossip and news. Soon, Colin knew, his mother would come to bed, settling down in the big hand-made fourposter which had travelled in the wagon and in which he had been born.

Normally, at this hour, all would have been asleep, for life was hard and a man, or boy, needed his rest. But the arrival of Uncle Zeke had thrown out the schedule so that tiredness was forgotten as the corn whiskey passed from hand to hand and the smouldering lamp threw shifting shadows on the rough walls of the cabin.

Softly Colin rose and, in the faint light streaming through the cracks in the door, examined his new weapon. It was a good gun, the best he'd ever handled, and he was impatient to try it out. Not tonight, that was impossible, but first thing in the morning he would rise and step down towards the creek and see if he could get a couple of wild ducks or some other tasty morsel to add to the monotonous diet of pork and beans.

But even to wait until tomorrow was hard. Surely there would be no harm in loading the gun ready for the coming day?

Colin was a boy, but on the frontier boys rapidly became men. He was no stranger to guns and could handle powder and ball as well as his seniors. From beneath his bed he dragged a box, took his spare cache of powder and carefully rammed home a measured charge in each barrel. He selected a bullet for the rifle, shook his head when he discovered that it was a little small, but patched it and rammed it home just the same. The shotgun held no difficulties; he had no buckshot but used instead a score of small birdshot. Carefully he crimped on the caps over the nipples, gently rested the hammers on the copper envelopes and, heart pounding with excitement, climbed back into bed.

Beside him, leaning against the wall, the polished barrels of his gift seemed to be the most precious thing in the whole world. More precious even than the gold Uncle Zeke was talking about in his deep, booming voice.

'Yes, sir,' he was saying. 'I tell you that there's gold in those hills and one day I'm going to find real pay-dirt.'

'That's what they all say,' said John. His voice was thick from the unaccustomed whiskey. 'I've seen them before, all the prospectors and hopefuls heading into the hills after El Dorado.

Sometimes they come back, sometimes they don't, but I've never met anyone yet who ever did more than wash a few ounces of dust from a creek or maybe find a few nuggets.'

'But the sign is there, John,' said Zeke. 'That dust was washed down from somewhere and the nuggets tell of a mother lode not too far off.' The fire hissed as he spat. 'I tell you the gold's there. One day someone will hit a bonanza and then you'll see this part of the territory spring into life.' He sucked thoughtfully at his teeth. 'I bet the Indians know.'

'Know what, where the gold is?'

'That's what I mean.' Zeke reached for the almost empty jug. 'They've lived in these parts for centuries, no one knows for just how long, and they must know where to find the yellow stuff.'

'I don't see that,' protested Matilda. 'If they knew where the gold was then why don't they mine it? They could buy blankets and food and guns and horses instead of begging and stealing the way they do. It don't make sense.'

'To an Indian it does,' said Zeke. 'They don't use money, Matilda, not as we do, and think of gold as yellow stone. To them it's useless, too soft to hold an edge and too heavy for ornaments. Anyways, stealing, to an Indian, is part of his way of life. They hold a horse thief in high regard.'

'I'd hold him high too,' said John grimly. 'As high as the highest branch of the nearest tree. Horse thieves should be strung up to dance in the wind.' He grunted as he thought about it. 'Anyway, why worry about the Indians? Dirty lot of savages, that's all they are.'

'Not so savage,' protested the prospector. 'I've lived in their lodges for a spell, before the young braves started mixing war paint that is, and they ain't so bad. Me and them used to get along real nice, still would I reckon if things would quieten down and the traders would stop cheating them and selling them whiskey. Whiskey's bad for Indians, John, sends them kill-crazy and half the time they don't know what they're doing when they're drunk. Seems to me as if the traders are to blame for the war drums beating, not the Indians themselves.'

'The way you talk scares me,' said Matilda nervously. She had a great fear of Indians. 'You think that there may be trouble?'

'Not the way you mean,' said Zeke comfortingly. 'A few warriors are after collecting coup, but that ain't nothing new. Thunder Cloud's a strong chief and he won't signal no uprising. I guess you can rest safe in your bed for a spell.' He chuckled but, after she had retired, became more serious.

'Didn't want to upset her, John, but if I was you I'd take to carrying a pistol when away from the house.'

'Like that?' John stared at the bowl of his pipe. 'I've never had no trouble with the Indians, Zeke. A little stealing in the early days but I stopped that. Why should they want to attack us?'

'A crazy Indian will attack anything,'

said the prospector. 'And a drunk Indian's a crazy Indian. I heard talk of a whiskey wagon in the hills, trading rot-gut for furs. That means trouble.'

'And you were attacked.' John nodded. 'You trying to scare me, Zeke?'

'Could I, John?'

'A man with a wife and son can scare easy.' John glowered into the dying fire. 'It's too lonely here for Matilda and she's right in what she says about Colin. He needs schooling. But I need him on the farm and there ain't nowhere I can send him.' He sighed. 'Things would have been different had there been others.'

Zeke nodded, not answering. For any frontier family a single child was disastrous. Labour was scarce and the only way a family could establish itself was by means of its own efforts. Large families were essential if the land was to be worked and the holding increased for, with the nearest neighbour some fifty miles away, each family was on its own.

The prospector yawned and stretched himself. He had ridden hard, eaten well and the whiskey and the warmth of the fire had made him sleepy. He yawned again as a coyote howled in the distance.

'Guess I'll turn in John. Same place?'

'If you want. I guess you could bunk down on the floor or on a heap of blankets if you wanted to.'

'Not for me.' Zeke rose. 'I'll sleep back of the stables. Couldn't drop off on a soft bed and walls sort of suffocate me.' He picked up his bedroll. 'See you in the morning, John. Sleep tight.'

John returned his farewell with a lift of his hand and sat for a while staring into the glowing coals of the fire. Almost he envied his brother. Zeke was free, as free as the wind as he rode through the hills on his search for gold. Maybe he wouldn't find it or maybe he would. If he did he would become rich overnight, far richer than any farmer and he wouldn't have spent years breaking his back trying to tame virgin soil. But on the other hand he wouldn't have had the comforts of a wife and the enjoyment of a son.

John shrugged, killed the lamp and made his way into the other room. Colin stirred as he passed but didn't wake. Matilda was already asleep. She turned as John climbed into bed, settling down again as he brushed her hair with his hard palm.

Within minutes his snores began to rumble like distant thunder.

It was the gun which woke Colin. He dreamed of it and turned restlessly on his bed then, without any apparent transition period, he found himself awake, ears straining for something he half-imagined he heard. Nothing but the sough of the wind came to his ears. Through the open door the faint light of the near-dead fire shone from the barrels of the weapon standing beside his bed. From the silence and the chill nip in the air he guessed that it was still a long way from dawn. Reaching beside him he lifted the weapon and let his hands caress the smooth steel. The temptation to slip outside and test the weapon was almost irresistible but he fought it down. Reluctantly he put aside the gun and, was just burying his head in the pillow, when he heard the mules.

It was a small sound but it jerked him immediately upright. From the stables came a stamping, a restless shifting and moving sound. The animals, Colin guessed, were restless. The cause could have been anything; most likely because of the strange mule, but also it could be a sign that the animals were in danger. Farm bred as Colin was he knew that such noises could not be ignored. His voice and presence could be enough to quieten the beasts and, if there was actual danger, he could attend to it.

Softly he slipped from his bed, pulled on his jeans, shoved his feet into his boots and, picking up the gun, headed from the cabin.

The stables were a few feet from the main structure, more of a lean-to than a separate building, closed by a flimsy door and giving little other than protection from the elements. The building held three mules and Colin soothed them, speaking quietly as he called them by name. They shifted in the darkness as they recognized his voice and in the fitful starlight, he could see their bulks. He called again, waited until they had settled down and was turning away when his nostrils wrinkled to a sudden odour.

It was unfamiliar and yet he had smelt it before. A sharp, acrid odour of rancid fat, the odour associated with burning animal-fat lamps — or Indians. Colin knew why Indians smelt that way, they were in the habit of smearing their bodies with grease, rubbing it in their tangled hair and on their garments. Indian odour was unmistakable and Colin thinned his lips as he automatically cocked the hammers of his weapon.

Indians were thieves and it was possible that a young brave was trying to steal a mule, some harness or anything else he could lay his hands on. Colin, even then, felt no real personal fear, most Indians had a healthy fear of the white man's guns and ran like the wind when discovered on a stealing expedition.

The boy never saw the shadow which rose from the ground behind him and the sharp-edged tomahawk which swung towards his skull.

Luck saved him. His foot turned as he moved and his ankle folded beneath him, throwing him down and to one side as the tomahawk hissed through the space where he had stood. Startled by the sound Colin turned, saw starlight reveal a hideously painted visage and, in sheer reflex, pressed the first trigger of his weapon.

Fire stabbed from the muzzle, illuminating the painted warrior and the sound of the ball as it smashed into the warrior's forehead was dreadful to hear. Echoes rolled from the sudden blast of the rifle and, for a moment, everything seemed to be frozen. Then the warrior screamed, dying as he fell. Shadows lifted to their feet as a circle of braves rose from their concealment and the air was torn by the terrible war whoop of the Sioux.

It was ghastly, that sound, a noise designed to paralyse the enemy with shock and fear and so render him helpless beneath the knives and tomahawks of the warriors. In the stable the mules kicked and reared and Colin could hear his father call out from the cabin. Then men were rushing towards him, the starlight glimmering from their weapons and again the weapon blasted in his hands.

It was answered by stabs of flame from behind him.

'Uncle Zeke!' Terrified, spattered with blood from the terrible effects of a full charge of birdshot fired into a leaping body at close range, Colin ran towards his uncle. 'Uncle Zeke, it's me!'

'Down.' Zeke sweated at the thought of how close he had come to killing his nephew. Tensely he gripped the boy by the shoulder and threw him behind a hummock. The long barrelled Colt in his hand roared again towards the Indians, their screams merging with the explosions.

'Pa!' Colin reared to his feet, the empty and useless weapon in his hands. 'Ma!'

'Down, you fool!' Zeke sucked in his breath as something whined towards them. 'You want to collect an arrow or a lance? Get down!'

'But Pa and Ma, they're alone.'

'Nothing we can do,' snapped Zeke. He fired twice more then he swore as the hammer clicked on an empty chamber. 'Let's run for it.'

'No!' Colin pulled away from his uncle. He stared towards the cabin now limned in flame. A shape staggered towards the door, clothes alight and screaming. An Indian leapt forward, steel flashing in his hand as his tomahawk buried itself in yielding bone. It lifted again, the blade dulled and his scalping knife flashed as he stooped over the silent figure. When he straightened again he held something in his hand.

'Scalped!' Zeke pulled at the boy. 'Don't look, son. Don't look!'

'That was Pa.' Colin felt sick.

'Don't look Colin!'

Sparks flared from the burning cabin as the flimsy roof collapsed and the circle of howling Indians, their painted bodies making them seem like grotesque figments of a nightmare, screamed and capered around the burning building. The mules had gone from the stable, taken away by the Indians, and a small group of them were scavenging around the area for what they could find. As yet, by sheer chance, none of them had stumbled on the two dead Indians Zeke had shot nor on those whom Colin had slain.

'Drunk,' said Zeke tensely. 'If they was sober we'd be dead now.'

'Ma!' Colin strained against the hand holding him down. 'Where's Ma?'

The wind brought his answer. A gust of it blew smoke and sparks towards them and, heavy on the odour of burning wood was another, more terrible scent. It was the scent of roasting meat and charred bone. It was the smell found around a campfire when the hunters burn the bones and entrails of their prey, but this time it wasn't the remains of an animal which were burning.

'Damn them!' Zeke stared helplessly at his pistol. 'No powder or ball, nothing. Who'd have thought they'd have attacked?'

It wasn't a question Colin could answer. Later he would wonder at the fates which had allowed him to escape the trap but now he could think of nothing but his dead parents.

'I should have known,' said Zeke, filled with self-remorse. 'I should have heard them, or smelt them.' He thrust the empty gun in its holster. 'I'm worse than an Indian,' he swore. 'Full of liquor and sleeping like a hog until your shots woke me.' He stared towards the flaming cabin and the group of questing Indians. 'Let's get out of here.'

Cautiously Zeke began to wriggle backwards away from the burning cabin, almost dragging the boy away with him. Colin acted as though half stunned, his white face seeming that of a boy near death. Only once did he make a protest.

'We can't leave them, Uncle Zeke.'

'What can we do?' The prospector squinted through the flame-shot darkness, his whisper tense with urgency. 'We've no powder or ball, nothing but the knife at my belt. There's a full dozen braves out there and all of them raging drunk. Hell, boy, if they catch us we'll die slow and nasty. Forget your Pa and Ma, they're dead. We've got to look after our own skins.'

He was brutal because he had to be brutal. Now was not the time for mourning and tears were a luxury. Later, he knew, he would get numb drunk in order to shut out the sight and sound and smell of what he had seen. But now he had to fight the impulse to rage among the Indians, knifing and clubbing until he fell. The boy was more important than vengeance.

He kept hold of Colin's arm, his fingers like steel as he drew further and further away from the cabin.

'Horses,' he whispered to the boy. 'They must have come on horses. They would have left them well away from the cabin for fear of dogs.' He swore with sudden bitterness. 'I told John he should have some dogs.'

'Bruce died,' said Colin dully. 'We didn't have a chance to replace him.'

'No sense in crying over that now.' Zeke lifted his head and stared about him. 'If I can locate the horses, kill the guard and get moving we stand a chance. Normally we wouldn't but those braves are so drunk they'll fall over themselves in the dark. Can you smell horses?'

Colin sniffed at the air trying, above the drifting scents of wood smoke and burnt flesh, to distinguish the animal odour of the wiry ponies the Indians rode. He stiffened at a more familiar odour.

'Indian smell.'

'Where?'

'That way.' Colin pointed. 'Pretty close.'

'Stay by me and use that gun as a club. If you see anyone smash their skull or jab the barrel in their stomach. Move fast and don't make more noise than you have to.'

Zeke's fingers dug again into the boy's shoulder as he led the way forward.

There were two guards. They stood just before the horses, their nostrils flaring and their eyes glistening as they stared at the burning cabin. Behind them, dim shapes in the starlight, the ponies waited with the trained patience of the Indian mounts. Colin sensed rather than saw his uncle rise, his knife-loaded hand darting forward and upwards, the keen steel ripping through

39

skin and muscle until it lodged in bone.

The Indian shrieked, twisting with pain and anger and he struck back at the white man beside him. The other warrior sprang forward, his hand snatching the tomahawk from his belt just as Colin stabbed forward with the empty gun. The barrel sank into the Indian's stomach in a vicious thrust which would have felled a white man. It didn't fell the Indian, his war whoop rang out in a savage burst of sound and the tomahawk lifted to split the skull of the boy. Zeke, seeing the danger, released his knife and sprang forward. For a moment the Indian hesitated between two foes and, in the split second, Colin smashed the gun down on the painted face.

'Quick!' Zeke snatched at reins. 'Up and get going.'

Colin searched for a stirrup, remembered that Indians rode bare back and felt his uncle boost him upwards. From the cabin yells answered the war whoop of the guard and lithe shapes came running towards the horses. Zeke swore with impatience, flung his leg across another mount and, screaming and yelling at the top of his voice, jabbed his heels into his mount's sides. Colin, clinging desperately to the shaggy main of his mount, followed his example while the rest of the horses, startled by the yells and screams, bolted into the night.

'Ride!' Zeke grabbed at the reins of Colin's horse. 'Hang on and ride for your life!'

'I can ride.' Colin drummed his heels against the pony. 'Where are we heading?'

'To the nearest homestead.' Zeke sucked in his breath as the ponies jolted over the rough trail. 'Keep going, Colin. Keep going!'

The boy bit his lip and did as he was told. Behind him the flames from the burning cabin faded into the distance and, high above, the moon rose to illuminate the trail. It helped, but not for long and with the coming of darkness again, the ponies slowed and stepped cautiously over the rough ground. Colin tugged at his reins when he heard a sigh and the sound of something falling.

'Uncle Zeke, you all right?'

'I'm all right.'

Colin slipped from his mount and ran to his uncle's side.

'I tell you I'm all right!' snapped the prospector. 'Just not used to riding, that's all. Let's get going.'

'Can't we rest? No one's chasing us.'

'They will be.' Zeke sounded grim. 'Come dawn and they'll be tracking us down for certain. They'll be sober by then and mean.' He grunted at the jolting of his mount. 'It's just that I ain't used to riding without a saddle. Know your way, Colin?'

'I think so. Come daylight I'll know it.'

'Good.' The sound of Zeke's breathing echoed above the dull thud of the unshod hoofs. 'Look, son.' he said suddenly. 'It might turn out that you'll have to make it alone. I've a few ounces of dust in a poke. I want you to take it. Here.'

His hands fumbled in the darkness and Colin felt a small leather bag pressed into his hands.

'Tuck it in your shirt, son, and guard it close.' Zeke coughed, swore, then his voice strengthened. 'You're 'most a man now, Colin, and you'll have to act like one. You've no kinfolk to help you now.'

'I've got you, Uncle.' Colin turned and stared to where Zeke loomed a dark shadow in the night. 'You ain't going to leave me, are you?'

Zeke didn't answer.

'Uncle Zeke, you ain't going to leave me.' Panic stirred deep inside of Colin. He was still young, little more than a boy and he'd just seen his parents brutally slain by Indians who, at this very moment, might be tracking him down. Zeke, to him, represented safety and comfort.

'I don't want to leave you, son,' said Zeke evenly. 'But sometimes a man

can't always do what he wants to do.'
He coughed and wiped his mouth
with the back of his hand. 'Hang on to
that gold, son, and take care of
yourself. You're a good boy, Matilda's
boy, she was a good woman too.' He
seemed to shake himself. For a while
they rode in silence, the ponies
stepping carefully towards the east.
Above their heads the stars wheeled
and turned as they had done for
countless years in the past. It grew
colder and Colin, thinly dressed as he
was, felt his teeth chattering.

'Let's rest a mite,' said Zeke. He
slipped from his mount and lay at the
side of the trail. 'Reckon it's safe
enough now. Come dawn make tracks
for safety, don't stop for nothing. Folks
will take care of you if you ask. You're
strong and can help on the farm. I
reckon you'll get along.'

Again that hint that he was to be
alone. Colin bit his lips against tears as
he thought about it, feeling the reaction
from the fight and the flight begin to

sap his courage. He tried to dissolve his fear in anger.

'Damn Indians,' he said. 'Dirty Sioux! I'll make them pay for what they did to Ma and Pa.'

Zeke sighed, not answering.

'I'll get my own back for what they did.' Colin felt tears sting his eyes. 'Scalping Pa and burning Ma. Dirty murdering scum! They ought to be killed, the lot of them.' He blinked towards his uncle. 'Ain't that right, Uncle Zeke?'

A sound like a moan answered him. Scared, the boy reached forward and rested his hand on the prospector's chest. It touched something wet and sticky and, in the starlight his hand showed an ugly darkness.

'Uncle!'

The wind moaned and a coyote howled in the distance. Or was it a coyote? Indians sometimes signalled to each other by means of animal cries.

'Uncle Zeke!' Colin shook the supine man. 'Can you hear me?'

Again the moan, a long, slobbering sigh which merged with the wind. Zeke was hurt, Colin knew it, the wetness could only be blood. He had been hit, maybe by an arrow or lance or more likely by the knife of the horse guard he had slain. He had hidden his wound, riding despite his loss of blood so as to guide the boy to safety. And suddenly his hints and meaning became clear.

'Don't die!' Colin felt fresh terror at the thought of the big, bearded jovial man shedding out his life in the empty dark. 'Don't leave me.'

He felt helpless, knowing there was nothing he could do until the light came and he could see the wound. So he waited, sitting by his uncle's side, shivering as the stars wheeled towards dawn and hoping all the time that he would not be left alone.

But when the dawn came Zeke was dead.

3

The year was 1859 and the burning of an isolated cabin was nothing unusual. The Indians were becoming restless and, fired by new leaders, armed with modern weapons they rose to make a futile stand against the advance of the white man. Futile because they were beaten before they started. But such small uprisings caused little comment. Other, greater events were shaking the country.

Down South a bearded fanatic led a small band against the government arsenal at Harper's Ferry. Their slogan was freedom for the slaves; the way they sought to gain that freedom was by bloody rebellion. John Brown failed in his plan and died on the scaffold but he lived on in song to fire the North against the slave-owning South. Talk of secession and the rumbling threat of war echoed from Maine to Florida, striking sparks wherever men gathered and creating hate between brother and brother.

Colin, taken in by a warm-hearted family, treated more like a son than the hired man he was supposed to be, was fifteen when the thunder of cannon at Fort Sumner heralded the outbreak of civil war. Abe Lincoln was immediately elected President, war-fever swept the land and the Blue and Grey met on the field of battle.

Two years later Colin decided to enlist in the Union Army.

'You sure you know what you're doing, Colin?' Jud Taylor, old, stooped, a withered hickory-stick of a man, squinted at the youngster from blurred eyes. 'You sure?'

'I'm sure.' Colin met the eyes of his benefactor. 'I'm going. Maybe I'll come back, maybe not.'

'It's the war,' sighed Sarah. 'Men killing each other all the time, what's to become of us all?' She needed no answer to her question. Two of her eldest sons had already died in the first days of conflict, two others, yet too young, waited impatiently and hoped that the war would last long enough so that they could earn glory. Now Colin was going and no one could stop him.

Nancy tried. Nancy was sixteen, a well-grown girl with long toffee-coloured hair and blue eyes which seemed to hold all the merriment in the world. She pressed Colin's arm, blushing a little, hoping that he would make things easier for her.

'You don't have to go,' she whispered. 'Pa needs help real bad and I'm admitting that I'll be missing you, Colin.'

'You'll forget.' Colin busied himself tightening the girths of his horse.

'I don't reckon that I can forget,' she said softly. 'Must you go?'

'Yes.' He stared down at her and read the message in her eyes. He wasn't surprised, folks married young in the West and false modesty belonged to the cities. Had things been normal he would have considered it. Had his own folks been alive it would have been the inevitable thing for him to do. But now he had no folks, no kin, nothing to tie his feet. A wife was something he could do without, had to do without for while he was free he was his own master. And he had never forgotten a night five years ago when screaming devils had danced around the burning cabin and the smell of his mother's burning flesh hung heavy on the air.

'You'll come back?' She stared up at him, her lips parted and the lines of her firm, young figure clearly revealed against the cotton dress that she wore. 'You'll come back, Colin?'

'No.' He hardened his heart against the pain in her eyes. 'Don't wait for me, Nancy. This is goodbye.'

He rode away on the horse he had bought with his earned money, a tall, shabby figure still wanting his full growth, but he rode as a man rides and the girl, looking after him with tear-filled eyes, could think of him as nothing other than a man.

But she knew that he would not return.

The war swallowed Colin as it swallowed so many others. He sold his horse and gear and donned the Union Blue. He learned to obey orders, to march, to live in dirt and filth. They tried to teach him how to use a rifle and pistol but he needed no teaching. Soon, because of what he was and what he wanted to become, he was singled out for special duties. Then he turned into a scout, creeping and crawling deep into the enemy lines, ready to kill if discovered or die if he had to. It was guerrilla war as divorced from the regular movements of the infantry and cavalry of the main armies. Colin was good at it.

'Man, you must have had a snake for a pappy,' said his captain one day. Nolan was a big man, a man who had risen from the ranks by the sheer force of his capabilities. That he wasn't given command of a regular patrol didn't worry him. He knew that his speech was uncouth, his manners more suited to the wagon line he had run before the patriotic fever had gripped him, and that he wasn't considered a gentlemen by the scented ladies of headquarters. He didn't care. He was happy when on a mission, wriggling like an Indian through the enemy lines, then to burn and kill and destroy in one of the constant raids which were sapping the strength of the South.

'We've got a big one coming up soon,' continued Nolan. 'I want ten men who can handle dynamite. I've picked the others, you want to come?'

'I can't handle the stuff, Captain.'

'You can learn.' Nolan was brusk. 'Klien will teach you. I want you to volunteer, Colin. I've got a feeling that I'll need you.'

Colin didn't answer. The war was dragging to a close and he was weary of the bloodshed. To him it seemed wrong that white men should slaughter each other while a common enemy waited to the West. And too many of the sights and sounds he had witnessed wakened unpleasant memories. The scent of roasting meat turned his stomach, even though it was a scrap of beef held on a ramrod over a camp fire. The rebel yell of the Confederate Army woke echoes of the Sioux war whoop. He didn't like the dirt and filth, real dirt and filth as against the normal dust and grime of farming. He hated the lice which fed on his body and earned rude comment at his insistence on bathing at every opportunity.

'You're the best scout I've got.' Nolan prodded at the fire before his tent. 'I've seen Indians at work and you'd hold your own with any warrior. How come you learned to do that, Colin?'

'It came natural, I guess.' Discipline was lax in the guerrilla patrols. The men lived hard and relaxed in the same way. They were a hard-bitten crew, mostly from the West and they valued their personal freedom too highly to pay lip-service more than they had to. Nolan understood them, he was one of them himself, but a West Point officer would have been shocked and horrified. But such an officer would never have been able to gain their loyalty.

'Natural?' Nolan shrugged. 'Maybe you're right. Some men can do it, other's can't.' He spat into the fire. 'This is a big one, Colin. The armies are getting ready for the deciding battle. If we lose this one then we could lose the war. Our job is to make sure that we don't lose.'

'Munitions?' Colin was soldier enough to fill in his own gaps.

'That's right. We've got to cut their line of supply. We do it by blowing up the railroad bridge at Twin Forks and if we time it right we'll blow up a munitions train at the same time. Better find Klien and have him show you how to handle dynamite.'

Klien was an old miner, a man who had both respect and understanding of the powerful explosive he had used before the war.

'Dynamite's funny stuff,' he said to Colin. 'You can burn it like a candle, hit it with a hammer, even shoot a bullet into it and it won't blow off. You need a detonator to make it do that.' He produced a stick of dynamite and a small detonator. 'See, you crimp on the fuse, push the fused detonator into the stick and now she's ready to blow. Fuse burns at about a foot every ten seconds.'

'Seems simple,' said Colin.

'Simple, like a snake,' agreed Klien. 'Don't treat this stuff with contempt. A lot of men have died that way and it was their own fault. The older dynamite gets the more touchy it becomes and temperature can do the same thing. You've got to be respectful with it all the time. If you are then it's safe.' He slipped a knife from his belt. 'Mostly we use a stick or several sticks, one detonator will do for as many as you like. But sometimes you may have to cut a stick, say for blowing out a tree stump or something like that. Then you treat it as if it were a candle.' The blade of his knife sliced through the stick of dynamite. 'Right. Now prime and blow this piece.'

Carefully Colin took the dynamite, a detonator cap and a length of fuse. He crimped the fuse to the cap, inserted the detonator into the dynamite and looked around to see where he should blow the explosive.

'Throw it in the creek,' said Klien. He gripped Colin's arm as the young man was about to light the fuse. 'Hold it!'

'What's wrong?'

'Check your fuse. It may be volleyed, that is the powder might be thin in one part so that the flame will either go out or leap forward too fast. If it goes out it doesn't much matter but if it volleys then you'll have it go off too soon.' His thick fingers ran the length of the waxen-white fuse. 'Seems all right. Let her go.'

Colin touched the end of the fuse to a brand, held on for a moment to make sure that the fuse was well alight, then flung it towards the creek. The explosion sounded like the roar of a cannon. Colin was surprised at the lack of apparent damage.

'She went off in the air,' said Klien. 'You've got to confine an explosion if you want to do damage. Otherwise it's just a big, empty bang.' He looked up as Nolan came towards them. 'He's all right, Captain.'

'Glad to hear it.' Nolan was obviously thinking of something else. 'Get your gear and make sure you forget nothing. We start at midnight.' He left Klien staring after him.

The journey to Twin Forks was similar to a dozen other journeys Colin had already made with the patrol. They rode as fast as horseflesh could bear them to the limit of their lines and then, moving at night, they passed into enemy country. They still wore their uniforms of Union Blue, to do otherwise would have meant getting shot or hung as a spy if captured, but they moved only with the utmost caution, guiding themselves by the stars, travelling fast and holding up during the day to eat and rest.

They were cheerful enough, the entire patrol looking on the mission as in the nature of an exciting experience. During the periods of rest Klien taught Colin more about the use of dynamite, telling him of its tricks and relative power. At night, with the young man questing ahead, they glided like soundless ghosts through a countryside which was torn and scarred by almost constant war. They reached the railroad on the dawn of the fifth day.

'This is it.' Nolan checked his maps and pursed his lips with satisfaction. 'We're a little too far to the west by about two miles. Klien, I want you to take a couple of men and head for the bridges. Set your dynamite and make sure that you get a train if you can. I'll take two men and head further west.

There's a junction about five miles down the line and we may as well destroy that too. The rest of the patrol can stay here with the horses.'

'You think that's smart?' Colin thrust himself forward. 'It's daylight now and this railroad will be guarded. A small party may manage to get through but only with luck. Try doubling it you're taking too big a chance.'

'What do you suggest?'

'Wait until night and then set the charges. We can be well away by the time they blow.'

'If they blow,' reminded Nolan. 'Someone may spot them or something else may happen. I don't trust those contact fuses Klien dreamed up. The dew is pretty thick around here and could damp the primers.'

'It won't,' said Klien. 'I've fixed them good.'

'You can't be sure.' Nolan hesitated. 'There's another reason why we can't wait. We're behind schedule and twenty-four hours could make all the difference.

We've got to wreck the line today.'

There was, as Colin could see, no further use for argument.

The horses had to stay hidden, that was obvious, and Nolan detailed a guard to take them into a small plantation. Klien, Colin and a heavyset man started off for the bridges at Twin Forks while the Captain selected a couple of men to make for the junction. His last words were prophetic.

'If anything should happen it's each man for himself. But don't let anything happen. This is war, you're armed soldiers in uniform, you have a right to kill, take prisoner and destroy enemy personnel and property.' He grinned. 'But maybe the Southerners won't see it that way. So be careful.'

Care, as Colin soon found, was essential. He was in the lead, guiding his two companions through a nest of underbrush a short way from the railroad, when he froze at the sight of grey uniforms. Klien crept quietly to his side.

60

'Anything?'

'Patrol.' Colin tensed as the mounted men rode towards their hiding place. Tensely the three men waited until they passed, the sound of their spurs and conversation echoing on the still, morning air. Another patrol rode along the permanent way searching, obviously, for signs of sabotage.

Silently the three men watched them ride down the tracks and out of sight.

'They know something,' said Klien sombrely. 'Some lousy spy has tipped them off. I hope that Nolan doesn't get caught.'

'That's his business.' Colin frowned in thought. 'But maybe you're wrong about them having been tipped off. It could be a routine patrol.' He started forward. 'Let's get on with the job.'

Twin Forks was a deep, swiftly-running river split in two by a long island and spanned by a pair of covered bridges. The bridges were built of wood, great thick timbers joined and strutted until they were as strong as the side of a hill. Klien sucked at his teeth as he stared at the structure, judging just where to set the dynamite so as to do the most damage.

'Nolan said for us to get a train,' reminded the heavyset man. 'How about setting the stuff under the rails with one of them trick fuses you made?'

'It wouldn't do the bridge much harm,' said Klien. 'It'd blow the train off the rails, sure, and maybe send it into the river, but it wouldn't do much damage to the bridge itself.' He narrowed his eyes as he examined the bridges. 'It'd be better if we could set the dynamite down among those struts. That way we'd rip the upper sections of the bridge to hell and get the train anyway.'

'That means climbing over the bridge,' said Colin. He pointed to where a twinkle of steel shone in the sunlight. 'There's a watch patrol stationed at the head of the bridge, they'd see us for sure.'

'Maybe, maybe not.' Klien rubbed at

his chin. 'A smart man could cover himself with the structure.'

'You've still got to blow the charges,' reminded Colin. 'You'll need a lot of fuse if you hope to get away before she blows. The longer the fuse the more chance the patrol will have of spotting it and cutting it before it's too late.'

'You're full of objections,' sneered the heavyset man. 'What you want for us to do, go back home without having a crack at the lousy Rebs?'

'I'm trying to be sensible,' said Colin. He wasn't annoyed at the heavyset man, he knew the words were dictated by nervous tension rather than any other reason. 'If we go out on the rails we'll be spotted. If we try to set the stuff under the bridge we'll have to use a long fuse and that means good timing. Seems there's only one real thing to do.'

'And that is?'

'Draw off the patrol.' Colin shrugged at their expressions. 'If it was dark it would be easy to blow the bridge and get away. But not in broad daylight, not unless we can do something to attract their attention and divert it from the bridge itself. I . . . '

'I've got an idea!' The heavyset man grinned. 'Should have thought about it before. What say I creep towards that patrol and toss a coupla sticks of giant powder in the middle of them? That would divert their attention for sure.'

'Let's not go off half-cocked on this.' Colin was the youngest of the three, scarcely more than a boy, but automatically he had taken command. 'The main thing is to crack the bridge. The second is to get a train.' He squinted down at the river below the hill on which they were hiding. 'Which way is the first train coming, east or west?'

'No idea.' Klien sucked at his teeth. 'What you thinking, Colin?'

'We could set a charge on the rails within the covered tracks on the first bridge and then blow up the structure of the other.' He shook his head.

'Forget that. The patrol is there to guard against sabotage inside the bridge itself, the risk wouldn't be worth it.' He sighed. 'Looks as if we'll have to do it the hard way. Wish I knew when a train was due.'

'Shouldn't be long,' said Klien. 'Not if that patrol was clearing and checking the tracks.'

'Let me blow them lousy Rebs to hell,' gritted the heavyset man. 'I can do it for sure.'

'Maybe.' Colin looked thoughtful. 'We haven't come all this way to ruin everything by haste. Let's take a scout to find out just what the opposition is.' He looked at Klien and the other man. 'You stay here, Klien, just in case we get caught. I'll take the east of the river and you take the west.' He looked at the heavyset man. 'Move slow and careful and don't take chances. We want information, not dead Rebs. Meet back here in an hour, less if you can. Let's go.'

It wasn't hard to creep through the

undergrowth. It was harder to remember that he was wearing a tell-tale uniform and that he would probably be shot on sight. Colin hugged the ground, his pistol loose in its holster and advanced until the scent of a cooking fire filled his nostrils. He crouched, easing himself to the shelter of a juniper bush, and listened to the confident voices of the guarding soldiers.

They were young, brash and over confident. They lounged around their cooking fire, impatient for hot coffee and biscuits fresh cooked in the portable oven. The man in Colin envied them their comfort while the soldier in him despised them for their carelessness. They were too confident that no one would ever attack them or the section of the line they were supposed to be guarding. They were due for a surprise.

The heavyset man had not yet returned by the time the youngster rejoined Klien. The old miner had been busy with his dynamite, cutting fuse and setting detonators. He started as Colin slipped beside him, his hand flashing to the pistol at his belt. He relaxed as he recognized the Union Blue.

'About a dozen men on the east,' said Colin. 'Young soldiers who know as much about soldiering as I do about flying. We could wipe them out with a surprise attack.'

'Is that what you aim to do?'

'No. We're here to destroy the bridges not to kill a handful of Rebs.' Colin stared towards the west side of the river. The heavyset man was coming towards them, the youngster could tell it by the tiny signs of his passage. He was breathing deeply when he finally reached the hiding place.

'Two men only.' He grinned. 'They was easy meat.'

'You killed them?'

'What else, they was the enemy wasn't they?'

'They were on guard,' said Colin. 'Probably due to be relieved. What happens when the relief finds them dead?' He didn't wait for the other's answer. 'I've got a plan. Klien and I will each take a load of dynamite and tackle the bridges. I'll take the east one and Klien the west. You take some short-fused sticks and create a diversion at the camp. You know what to do?'

'I know, I've done this before.'

'See that there's no mistake. If I miss my guess this area is lousy with Confederate troops and they'll come running at the sound of the explosions. So don't move too fast. Hold back until Klien and I have had a chance to set the charges and get away. If necessary don't make a move at all but, if they've spotted us, then let them have it fast and hard. Understand?'

'I know my business.' The heavyset man accepted the primed sticks of dynamite from the miner. He took a short cigar from his pocket and slipped it between his lips. Carefully he lit it, shielding the flame of his match. The cigar, Colin knew, was solely in order that the heavyset man could touch off the fuses of his crude bombs.

He grinned at his companions and adjusted his weapons.

'Do a good job,' he said easily. 'I'll try and make it back to the horses but if I don't I'll see you in hell.'

He vanished with a faint rustling of leaves.

4

The river was wide and deep, the current fast so that the water dashed itself into whiteness against the thick pilings of the bridge. Colin, hunched down at the foot of those pilings, looked for Klien and failed to see him. He was not surprised. Both men had separated when still high on the hill and each was making his own way as best he might. The miner, like Colin, had probably climbed down to the foot of the bridge in order to climb the structure to place his explosives. Colin hoped that the heavyset man would hold his hand until the last minute.

Climbing the structure of the bridge was not too difficult but it had its dangers. The wood near the water was slimy and damp. Higher it was better but it was almost impossible to avoid exposure to watchful eyes. Colin climbed towards the track above, trying to keep the thick timbers between himself and the camp he had spotted. Once he thought he saw the flash of sunlight on a carbine barrel and froze, pressing himself against the timbers of the bridge. He began to move only after he caught a glimpse of a figure on the other bridge. Klien was either careless or heedless of his danger.

His plan had been made before he had started to climb. Several timbers met in a junction midway along the span of the bridge and there he was going to set his explosives. He had barely reached it when he heard the yelled shout of a challenge. It was followed by the immediate crack of a rifle.

'Halt! You on the bridge, halt or we fire!'

Colin froze. Movement, he knew, was the worst thing to betray him so he hugged the timbers and cursed his uniform which made poor camouflage.

But it was not him the guards had seen.

Klien had been over confident. He stood on a cross member, hugging the dynamite under his jacket, and ran towards shelter as lead chipped splinters from the beams around him. The guards were excited, too excited to take proper aim, but it was only a matter of time before Klien was hit.

It was then that the heavyset man took a hand. He grinned as he touched a fuse to his cigar and, with one clean swing of his arm, tossed his bomb into the centre of the camp below. He followed it by another, a third, then ducked as ruptured air and blasting flame vomited from the ground. The roar of the explosions was followed by screams and a horrible moaning from men badly injured and unable to make sense of what had happened.

'How'd you like that, Rebs?' The heavyset man jumped to his feet, his remaining stick of dynamite in his hand. 'Like some more? Here it comes.'

Deliberately he lit the remaining fuse, swung his arm, then tossed the white, greasy, innocent-seeming stick towards the shambles below. He dived towards the ground as it disrupted in flame and violence, then raced towards the camp, his long-barrelled Navy Colt in his hand, intent on finishing the slaughter the dynamite had caused.

Shots lanced towards him, the whining death from a dozen carbines, and he halted, his thumb jerking at the hammer of his Colt as he returned the fire. Too late he realized the trap he had fallen into. The camp had only held a part of the guard detail, the rest were scattered along the hill, and, worse the patrol which had ridden down the track had returned. He was one man against over a score and the end was inevitable.

Colin, crouched on the east span of the bridge, heard the thunder of guns, the high-pitched Rebel yell, then a sudden silence. Desperately be climbed higher, racing against time and certain death as he struggled to place his dynamite.

Klien, too, had heard the explosions, the shots and the silence and he knew what they meant. He, himself, had been spotted, the shots which had chipped splinters from all around him was proof of that. His life, he knew, was forfeit, but he could still carry out his mission. He crouched on the bridge and stooped over the lethal package he carried. Desperately he tore at the fuses, biting the long length through with his teeth and so shortening the burning time. From a pocket he took a length of whipcord and began to lash the dynamite to the wooden structure. He fumbled in his pockets for matches, found them and rasped one on the side of the box. The lucifer fumed, smouldered and then went out. He cursed as he fumbled for another.

The bullet caught him just as he was about to light the fuse.

It was as if a clenched fist had smashed between his shoulders, the impact so great that, before he could recover his balance, he was tumbling towards the water below. Behind him, still resting on the bridge, the dynamite showed white against the sun-blackened wood.

'Got him!' Crouched on the bridge Colin could hear the triumph in the voice on the track above. 'Good shooting, sergeant.'

'Wish I could say the same about these so-called soldiers they had guarding the bridge,' said a deeper voice. 'They had him spotted before the explosions wiped out the camp.' He swore with a terrible intensity of emotion. 'The damn Yankees! Over a dozen of our boys torn apart by their hell-powder. Didn't even have a chance to defend themselves. That ain't war, major, it's murder!'

'The attacker was wearing full uniform,' reminded the major.

'So what?' The sergeant was bitter. 'Does that make everything all right? Over a dozen dead, more injured and the railroad in danger. Me, I like my wars to be decent. These damn Yankees will be killing women and babies next.'

'You're an idealist, sergeant.' The major spoke with a tired wistfulness. 'There is no glory in war and there is nothing to be proud of in civil war which is the worse form of war there can be. Women and babies, you say? Maybe we'll live to see that too. Maybe we'll live to envy those who died in the explosion, at least they died quick and easy.'

'I've never heard you talk this way before, sir.'

'No? Well, maybe not. But then I've never had my only son killed before, sergeant. The telegram arrived last night; he was killed in the attack on Jacksonville. A thing like that makes a man think, sergeant.'

'Yes, sir. I suppose it does.' The sergeant did not seem to know what to say. Enlisted men could hardly show sympathy with their superior officers even if they felt it. Colin heard the rasp of boots above as the sergeant shifted his position on the track. 'Guess we'd better send some men down to remove that dynamite, sir.'

'Of course. Send a full detail to search both bridges and another to check the track. I'll send word to the junction to scour the countryside. Those men couldn't have been alone, the rest of their party must be around here somewhere. And sergeant — '

'Yes, sir?'

'Hurry the search. The limited is due through here soon.'

'Yes, sir.' Boots rasped again as the man saluted and his deep voice yelled quick orders to the soldiers on the hill. A party of them broke away and moved towards the river while others began to examine the railroad track for signs of sabotage. Colin, crouched beneath the track, knew that it could only be a matter of minutes before he was discovered and shot down.

What he had to do he had to do fast.

Carefully he moved so as to give

himself room in which to work. From beneath his tunic he took the dynamite, the waxen sticks already tied in a compact bundle. Hastily he searched the timbers for a good place in which to plant the charge, knowing that unless it were placed correctly it would do little more than superficial damage. A few feet away one of the main timbers supporting the track above met crossbeams in a vital junction. Slowly he began to edge his way towards it.

Below him the grey uniformed figures of the Confederates had reached the bridges and were climbing upwards, searching each timber as they climbed. Others, their eyes watchful, stood on the side of the hill, their carbines in their hands. Colin, sweating with anticipation of a bullet, moved slowly and carefully towards the selected place, the lethal bundle gripped in his trembling hands. He reached it, set down the dynamite and took a length of cord from his pocket. He was lashing the bundle into place when he heard the first shout.

'Hey! There's someone on the bridge. Another damn Yankee, by God!'

A carbine sent echoes from the hills as the soldier fired towards the shape he had spotted and lead made an ugly sound as it buried itself in wood. A second shot whined thinly as it missed the crouching figure by an inch, then came a rattle of fire as the soldiers took quick aim and fired with desperate impatience. That very impatience saved Colin's life.

He was a small target, almost totally shielded by the timbers behind which he crouched and the soldiers were too eager to bring him down. A good marksman, taking his time, would have downed Colin at the first shot, but these raw troops were neither good marksmen or in full command of their nerves. They knew that the figure was that of an enemy, they guessed what he was doing and the memory of the roar of shattering dynamite was too recent in their memories. So they blasted the bridge with lead depending on sheer volume of fire-power to do what a single shot could have done.

The sergeant, who could have done what his troops could not do, was too far out of the line of fire to do more than yell harsh orders.

'Take your time, dammit! Aim real careful and squeeze on the trigger. Hell, are you trying to frighten him to death?' The thud of his boots as he raced towards the end of the bridge so as to get a clear shot vibrated the timbers against which Colin crouched.

The youngster took no notice. For some reason he had gained a remarkable calmness, and his fingers, as he lashed the dynamite into place, were sure and steady. He was aware of the bullets splintering the timbers around him, the sharp, angry whine as they ricochetted from the wood, the distant reports of the carbines, but only as something remote and distant. He tied the last knot, stooped and bit the fuse until barely a couple of inches remained and, slipping the pistol from its holster glanced down at the river below.

It would be a difficult jump. He had to spring clear of the timbers and make sure he hit the water down-current from the bridge, but there was no alternative. To leave a safe length of fuse would mean that the soldiers, even now climbing towards him, would have time to tear it free. He could, of course, fire a bullet directly at the detonator, but Colin was a soldier, not a fanatic. He wanted to destroy the bridge but he wanted a gambler's chance of life, too.

Lead plucked at his sleeve and something jarred his foot. A bullet had struck his heel. He glanced down, aimed his pistol so that the flame of the discharge would fire the fuse, and tensed his finger around the trigger.

A hand clawed at his foot almost pulling him off balance and a soldier, his face white with strain, swore horribly as he tugged at the ankle, trying to heave himself upwards. He held no weapon, he had needed both hands in order to climb, and now he teetered on the edge of the beam, one hand clutching Colin, the other reaching for a new hold.

'Damn Yankee!' He snarled like an animal as he clawed his way upwards. 'Damn . . .'

He stiffened, his face registering shocked surprise and from his open mouth spurted a thick stream of blood. A shot from the soldiers below had struck him in the back of the neck. His fingers, suddenly lax, slipped from Colin's ankle and he fell, vanishing suddenly from the edge of the beam.

A yell of rage echoed from the hills and the firing redoubled. Colin crouched, poised his feet, and, aiming his pistol, pressed the trigger. Immediately he jumped, thrusting from the bridge with the full strength of his legs as he hurled himself away from the packed dynamite. For an instant everything seemed to have frozen so that he hung in mid-air like a trapped bird. Then he was falling . . . falling . . . falling to the brown, rushing torrent below. His pistol slipped from his hand, his tunic billowed about him and the world seemed to be spinning before him. The bridge, the hills, the river, the bridge again, and then the hills spotted with white faces and little spurts of flame from hastily aimed carbines.

One of those hastily aimed bullets, either by luck or judgment, found a target. Colin jerked as searing pain tore at his back then, before his eyes, the bridge seemed to dissolve in slow motion, a great ball of flame erupting from the dynamite and great timbers seeming to float lazily in the air. The following roar of the explosion was lost as he hit the water.

He landed badly, feeling the breath knocked from his lungs as he hit the water, and then he was fighting for life as the current pulled at him and the brown torrent thrust itself into his mouth and lungs. Desperately he clawed his way to the surface, the pain in his back a living thing, and gulped air as sunlight struck his eyes. Debris fell around him, broken timbers and splintered wood, sleepers from the torn tracks and twisted lengths of rail. They plunged into the water sending up great showers of spray and among them Colin was an insect in a storm. He fought to remain afloat, his uniform dragging him down and the current making a mock of his strength.

Then something smashed against his skull and the world vanished into oblivion.

5

The tide of war had turned against the South and the memory of Sherman's 300-mile march across Georgia was a sickening thing in the minds of those who battled beneath the Stars and Bars of the Confederacy. Chivalry, for so long the pride of the South, was wearing thin, and hunger, want and physical misery had engendered a hatred of the Northern Armies who were pressing so close.

That hatred was reflected in the attitude of the men who wore grey. No longer were prisoners treated as unfortunate equals — if prisoners were still taken. Civil war had reached its true bitterness so that men who spoke the same tongue, shared the same heritage and who had been born in the same land hated each other as if they were races apart. And now Sherman was repeating his ghastly march in a second triumphal passage of the Carolinas and the grim smoke, of burning mansions, was heavy in the sultry Southern air. The war, so those who knew said, was almost over. The South was facing defeat and soon it would be finished.

But for some the war was far from over.

Luck saved Colin from a watery grave, luck and the dying chivalry of the major commanding the guard detachment who had ordered his rescue. He was dragged from the river, a great bruise on the side of his head and the bones of his left arm broken in three places. He was also wounded in the back and his impact with the water had covered his flesh with a tracery of welts and bruises so that he resembled a man who had been flogged with chains. But he was still alive.

'Kill him!' The sergeant, his face torn by splintered wood, scowled down at the hated blue uniform. 'Shove him back into the river and let him die.'

'No.' The major was firm. 'He is an enemy, yes, but a uniformed enemy and he is entitled to the usages of war.' His face darkened as he stared at the ruined bridge. 'He's done the cause more damage than a platoon of night-riders, but in that he only carried out his duty. He is a brave man, sergeant, let us treat him as such.'

So Colin was reluctantly carried to a military hospital and handed over to the care of a surgeon.

It was like an entry into hell.

Things were short in the Confederacy, and medical supplies were at a premium. Union wounded were herded together and given what attention could be spared from the mounting demands of the Confederate troops. It was not deliberate cruelty but death, for many of the wounded, would have been a mercy.

The surgeon in charge was an old man, too old for active duty and too old to do more than trust in God to do what the lack of medical supplies could not do. He was skilled and did what he could but at times, especially during the hours of uneasy sleep he managed to snatch from time to time, he would wake, sweating, the screams of the poor devils he treated ringing in his ears. For there were no anaesthetics, no clean bandages, no drugs to ease pain. Nothing but skilled speed in amputations and the cauterising tar which was smeared on bleeding stumps to stop the flow of blood and sterilize the wound.

Operations in the military hospital were things dreaded and to be feared as the ante-chamber of the Devil.

Colin was fortunate in that he was unconscious when they set his arm and he remained unconscious as the tired, over-worked orderlies prepared him for the operation to remove the bullet from his back. Even then he struggled to awareness as the probes searched for the bullet and the sting of the iodine was a naked agony. Then, the surgery completed, he was left to live or die as fate and his own constitution might dictate.

Sherman smashed his way through the Carolinas before Colin's battered body lost the traces of injury. The cast was removed from his arm on the day President Lincoln died to an assassin's bullet. He was able to walk without too much pain when the final, startling news came through that Jeff Davis had been captured and that the four-year long civil strife was over. The North had won and the once proud Confederacy was humbled into the dust. That was the 10 May, 1865, and Colin was almost nineteen years old.

The hospital went wild at the news, prisoners sat up in their cots or, if they had no cots, heaved themselves upright on the floor and forgot their wounds in the knowledge that the war was over. The air hummed with talk, of plans of family reunions, of sweethearts who were waiting and of kinfolk they would meet. Colin took no part in the talk, he was alone as few of the others were alone. He had no kinfolk, no family, not even a sweetheart, though at times he thought of Nancy. He dismissed such thoughts. The war had unsettled him and in the crucible of combat his resolve had been strengthened. Settling down was not for him. He had no roots and no desire to grow any. He wanted only to get away from war and bloodshed and pain. He wanted the clean sweep of open spaces, the fresh wind in his face and the open sky above him. He hated the scent of cannon smoke and burning, the stench of blood and the cries of pain. He wanted peace.

But peace had to wait. The war was over, yes, but it still was not a matter of just catching a horse and riding home. His wounds had not yet wholly healed and there were others to attend to. Captain Nolan for one.

Colin had been startled to find the captain in the same hospital. His rank had entitled him to better treatment but that fact had been forgotten or ignored in the final days of the war. Colin found him lying on a cot in a rear section of the mansion which had been taken over to house the wounded. He greeted Colin with a smile and tried to sit upright in the bed. He made hard work of it, his left arm had been amputated from the elbow.

'Colin, good to see you.' He ran his tongue over lips cracked and dry with fever. 'Thought they'd got you for sure.'

'They got the rest, I was lucky.'

'Did you get the bridge?'

'Yes.' Colin saw that the officer wanted more information. 'Klien tried and died. The other man created a diversion and I was lucky. Even at that it was a close thing.'

'They were expecting us,' said Nolan grimly. 'We were attacked a mile from the junction and without horses what could we do?' He winced as he tried to change position. 'I held out until I was shot, then surrendered.' He swore with remembered bitterness. 'We wore uniforms, weren't spies, but those Rebs treated us worse than dirt. They hung the other two, would have strung me up, too, but some fancy officer came along and stopped them. Even at that they refused treatment for my arm.'

He saw Colin glance towards the stump.

'It went bad on me,' he explained. 'Started to rot so they cut it off.' His lips thinned at the memory. 'You know how they operate in here? They take a man and hold him down. Then they cut off his arm. Then they smear it with hot tar.' Great beads of perspiration dewed his forehead. 'Hell, I've seen Indians torture their captives but they could learn a thing or two from a place like this.'

'It's over now,' soothed Colin. 'All over.'

'Yes,' said Nolan. 'That's right, isn't it?'

Colin nodded.

'And now what?' said the captain. 'I'm no longer fit for the army, not that they would have kept me on anyway, too rough for the ladies and those snotty lieutenants from West Point. But what am I supposed to do now? I can't handle a team with only one arm. I can't tend store or keep books. I can't go prospecting.' He beat his right hand on the filthy blanket which covered him. 'Hell, Colin, what can I do?'

It was a question the young man could not answer.

'It's no good staying in the East,' said Nolan. 'I've had enough of the East anyway. Maybe I can talk the army into keeping me on. There's a lot of forts in the West and maybe they'll give me a job at one of them.' His shoulders slumped in resignation. 'Why kid myself? What chance do I stand with only one arm and no education? There'll be dozens of West Pointers lining up for anything that's going, all the regular army men with pull and the right connections, they'll get all the plums.'

'It might not be so bad,' soothed Colin. He could see that the captain was racked with fever and more than inclined to be delirious. 'They'll probably send someone down here to arrange transportation home, pay us back pay, things like that.' He dipped a rag in the dirt-encrusted water-jug, wrung it out and wiped Nolan's sweating features. 'You just take things easy.'

'I know the West,' said Nolan suddenly. 'I drove wagons all over the area from Fort Laramie to Independence. I was in Denver when they hung John Brown and that's a growing place. They found gold there, did you know that? Maybe I could go back that way, open a saloon, maybe, do something like that.' His enthusiasm mounted. 'One arm wouldn't matter then. I could hire me a few boys to run the place and just keep an eye on things. Sure, that's the idea. I've had too much sweat and blood, now I should take things easy for a spell. Let others do the work while I sit back and get rich. Sure, that's what I'll do.'

Colin left him mumbling to himself,

his thin cheeks flushed with fever, his eyes too bright as he built himself mental dreams of a life of ease. They would remain dreams, Colin knew; men don't get rich by talking about it and they don't get rich by letting others do the work. But if the captain could escape from harsh reality into a fantasy of his imagination he saw no reason to stop him. The hospital was a place no man in his right mind would want to stay in, anyway.

But Nolan had disturbed him. For the first time Colin gave thought to his own future. He was footloose, rapidly gaining his old fitness and had had the taste of adventure. For a time he toyed with the idea of staying with the army but dismissed the thought almost at once. He had had enough of discipline and the stupidity of war. He wanted personal freedom. And yet what to do?

A grizzled oldster supplied the answer. In many ways he reminded Colin of his Uncle Zeke. He, too, had been a prospector until patriotism had swept him into the army, there to lose the sight of one eye and the use of one leg. He sucked at his toothless gums and squinted at the young man from his single remaining eye.

'Go west,' he said. 'Nothing else for a youngster to do. There's land out there and room to move around. There's gold, if you can find it, and plenty of game if you can't. A man can sleep with a full belly no matter what. All he needs is a good rifle, a couple of Colts and a horse. Why, if I was twenty years younger I'd have had more sense than to put on uniform.' He spat thoughtfully at a cockroach. 'Seems like a man loses his senses as he gets old. Me, I've got nothing to look forward to now unless I can get me a job in some livery stable. Know anyone who wants a good livery man?'

'Not me, Pop.'

'No, I guess not.' The toothless gums worked on imaginary tobacco. 'Any notion of how long we'll be kept here?'

Colin could answer that. He had

listened to the gossip and had spoken with the officer in charge of the hospital.

'A man will be coming down to pay us off within a few days,' he said. 'Those who want discharge can have it. The badly wounded will be taken care of. Everything will be cleaned up.'

'I've got plenty of back pay coming,' said the oldster. His eye glowed at the thought of pleasures to come. 'Me, I aim to enjoy things a bit!' What you going to do?'

'No idea.'

'You going west?'

'California, you mean?'

'Sure, you won't be the only one.' The oldster chuckled. 'Hell, it'll be like old times again. You'll see if I ain't telling you right. The Californian Fever will get hold of them and they'll be making tracks west.'

'Who?' Colin was interested.

'Who? All of them. The Southerners without homes and the Northerners who have nothing else to do. It'll be like

1846 all over again. There's free land for the taking out there, son, and that's a thing which will draw a man back from hell if he's that kind of a man.'

The old man spoke more truly than he knew. A sense of restlessness had seized the east and already wagon trains were lumbering out from Independence, that old springboard for the Western movement. The cry was all for free land, the rich, rolling acres of the virgin prairie and the lush slopes beyond The Rockies. But now there was a greater spur to the Westerners. Gold had been found in California and the fever of the yellow metal had taken those to whom free land meant nothing. Rumour, travelled back on the rare mails carried by couriers, had enlarged what was to be found at the diggings so that men believed all they had to do was to sink a pick in the soil and pick up great nuggets of solid gold. Land and gold fever was sending wagon train after wagon train across the prairies along the old trails to the West.

'I'd like to go west again,' said the oldster. 'I'd sure like to taste buffalo tongue again.' He smacked his lips. 'That's real eating, son. Tongue and maybe a bit of liver.' He sighed. 'Guess that I'll never see the herds again.'

'The buffalo herds?'

'Sure.' The old man blinked his eye. 'Thought you was from the west yourself, son? Mean to say you ain't seen the buffalo?'

'My folks settled just west of Missouri,' said Colin. 'We had Indians but I can't remember seeing buffalo.'

'Then you've missed something.' The oldster wiped his mouth with the back of his hand. 'Why, I remember them so thick they was like fleas on a blanket. You could have shot blind and still brought down a cow or maybe a bull. Hell, until you seen the buffalo you ain't seen the West.'

'Tell me more,' said Colin.

'Ain't that much to tell. A smart man with a little money could make himself a fortune shooting buffalo. The hides make good robes and the meat can be dried. Seems that I heard tell of the railroad companies wanting meat for their labour gangs or if you don't hanker for that then you could just collect for the hides.' A wistful expression entered the old man's remaining eye. 'A youngster could do worse than make himself a buffalo hunter. Yes, sir, I'd do it if I had two eyes and two legs which worked.' He sighed. 'But what's the use of talking? I'm like a broken down old mule, the spirit's there but the body ain't.'

Colin left him staring forlornly at the hickory shaft which had replaced his left leg from the knee down.

True to rumour the hospital had a visit from a representative of the Northern Army. He was a brusque civilian who had a job to do and who wanted to get it done. Regular soldiers were ordered where to report, and the men who had enlisted for the duration were given their discharge papers, back pay and a ticket to their home town.

Colin, who had no home town, asked for and received a ticket to Independence, Missouri. The old man's words had fired his imagination and he wanted to see some of the wagon trains the old man had talked about. Nolan, much to his surprise, was given the chance of remaining with the army.

'Seems as if they want men at Fort Dacre and they ain't particular about me having only one arm.' He sighed. 'Not that the fort is a good one, from what I can learn it's little more than a trading post for Indians with a handful of troops to keep order. But I'll be doing useful work and I'll get by.'

'That's the main thing,' agreed Colin. 'Still, I'm glad to hear that you're settled.'

'Wish you could come with me,' said Nolan suddenly. 'Why don't you? The fort is attached to a reservation so there won't be too much to do. I could use a good man though, someone who can hunt and track and use his head.'

'Why?'

'I just figure that a man like that is good to have around.' Nolan was dodging the question. 'All right,' he said as Colin remained silent. 'I'll tell you why. I ain't foolish enough to think that they're giving me this post out of charity. The way I see it is that they're doing it because no one else wants it. If it's what I think it is then there'll be dirty work to be done. It's a reservation, that I know, and those reservations are under the direct control of an Indian Agent. Some of them are honest, most aren't, and at times the Indians kick up rough. Troops are there only to keep order, order as laid down by the Agent. He's elected by the government and there ain't nothing anyone can do against him and still keep his job. But you aren't army and you will be a free agent.' He shrugged. 'Call it insurance, Colin, but I'd like to have at least one man I can trust within call.'

'You'll get by,' said Colin.

'You think so?' Nolan did not sound too certain.

'I know so.' Colin stared distastefully around the hospital. 'You're feeling low what with your arm and everything. Things will seem better when you get a horse between your knees again. It'll work out all right.'

'I hope so.' Nolan rubbed thoughtfully at his chin. 'What you aiming to do, Colin?'

'Look around for a spell, see what's going.'

'And then?'

'Maybe I'll try buffalo hunting.' Colin stared at the officer. 'Or maybe I'll go back to where I used to live.'

'I thought that your folks were all dead?'

'Maybe that's why I'd like to go back.'

'Maybe.' Nolan leaned back on his pillow. His eyes were shrewd as he stared at the youngster. 'How old was you when your folks died, Colin?'

'Twelve, why?'

'Indians?'

'That's right.'

'At twelve things make a deep impression. Would you be thinking of maybe going back to settle accounts with the Indians who did it?' His voice sharpened at the youngster's expression. 'I thought so. Don't do it, son. It's a waste of time.'

'Did I say it was in my mind?'

'You didn't have to. We've been together for most of two years and I don't ride with a man I don't know. I've studied you, watched you around the camp fires and seen the way you act. You've been training for something, maybe you don't even know just for what yourself, but that's what you've been doing.'

'You're crazy!' Colin made as if to rise and leave but Nolan caught his arm.

'I ain't crazy. You can handle a rifle better than most and better than any soldier. You can use a Colt, too, and you can draw from an open holster.' He chuckled. 'I know. Smiling Joe taught you and you paid him in whiskey and tobacco for the lessons. And you can track like an Indian. Kids do things for a reason, Colin, even though they might not know just what that reason is. You saw your folks die and saw the Indians that did it. Now you don't like Indians. Am I right?'

Colin remained silent.

'You don't have to answer. Is that why you won't come with me? Because part of my job will be to look after the reservation Indians?' Nolan nodded. 'You're young, Colin, and even though you look a man maybe you ain't quite grown up. Indians are like white men, some are bad, some are good. You fought the Confederates and saw your comrades dying but do you hate all the South?'

'That was different.'

'How was it different?'

'That was war, it was them or us in fair fight.'

'And to the Indians it was war, them or you.' Nolan settled back in his cot. 'I've been West and I know the Indians.

They just want to be left alone but we won't leave them alone. Fort Dacre for example, the reservation for the Arapahoes. You know what the territory is like there? Swamp, that's what, an Indians' grave. So maybe they want to cut loose and go back home and, if they do, then I'll have to stop them. I can't do it with talk, it'll have to be done with lead and a rope. You figure that they'll like that?'

'I'm not arguing.'

'Sure you're not, but listen all the same. So I hang a few and shoot a few and make them good Indians. Then what happens? They break out again and take their revenge by burning up a few homesteads and collecting a few scalps. Can you blame them?'

It made good sense but Colin did not want to listen to it. Nolan had surprised him by his shrewd assessment of his motives. Never once, even to himself, had he admitted that he hated Indians. He had not even seen an Indian since the night they had burned the cabin and thought that he had pushed the incident into the back of his mind. But now that the captain had spoken he could see the truth in what the other had said.

Something had made him perfect himself in the use of weapons. At first he had thought that it was to make himself a better soldier but now he began to have doubts. The West was wild, lawless, a place where a man carried his life at his belt and death came to those who were slow on the trigger.

'Don't do it, Colin,' whispered Nolan. His fever had returned and he was still weak. 'Don't waste your life on the vengeance trail.'

'I won't,' promised Colin, and he meant it. But waste was something to be defined by each man to himself.

He left Nolan and went from the hospital to think. The captain was right and the old man was right, the West was the place for a young man to go. Now that the Indians had been granted lands and reservations it seemed as if the old troubles were over. Wagon trains should have no trouble crossing the prairies and California was a land of promise.

To Colin, now used to the east, it seemed as if nothing could trouble the flow of traffic across the continent.

He was wrong.

6

Colin rode into Independence two years after leaving the hospital. During that time he had roved down into Mexico, headed into Texas and worked for a spell at handling the huge herds of cattle which had accumulated during the war. Despite the vast herds, poverty was apparent south of the Red River. The war had cut off trade and the cattle barons found themselves in the position of owning thousands of head of cattle but with little money to pay their hands. Jeff Stangler had tried to ship some of his beef up to the railhead and had lost cattle, men and almost his own life in a savage brush with the roving bands of self-appointed border guards who demanded tribute before allowing the herds to pass.

But cowpunching, Colin found, was

not for him. It was a dreary, monotonous, hard life broken only by the wild sprees at the end of round-up or a successful drive, neither of which was apparent. Sooner or later the deadlock would be broken and the great cattle drives begin again but he couldn't wait until that happened. Down in Texas he had heard of the streams of immigrants heading towards the gold fields of California and decided to attach himself to a train so as to see the new lands for himself.

There were two ways by which a man could gain passage across the continent. If he had money he could buy or build a wagon, buy oxen to draw it and take his possessions with him. Or he could hire himself to a train making the journey or to a family in need of extra help. Colin had little money, no desire to build a wagon and few possessions to take if he did. So he rode into Independence with the idea of finding a train in need of help.

A livery stable accepted his horse and

the livery man, a wrinkled oldster with a straggly beard directed the young man to the Last Chance saloon as the best place to meet the wagoners. There was nothing strange in that, saloons, in the West, were the social centres and common meeting ground of all the diverse types thronging the frontier. Here were to be found sober, respectable businessmen, hard-riding scouts and mule skinners, wagon drivers, professional gamblers, prospectors looking for a grub-stake and the dozen and one other types who either lived in or were passing through town.

'I reckon you'll find a coupla wagon bosses in there,' said the livery attendant. 'I did hear tell that Mark Longdon was looking for a couple of handlers for his party. Maybe you'd like to look him up?'

'Thanks.' Colin flipped the man a silver dollar. 'Take care of my horse, will you.'

'Sure.' The old man grinned at the touch of the silver. 'You want I should feed him grain?'

'Yes, but don't overdo it. I don't want to get him in bad habits.' Both men laughed at the joke and Colin headed towards the Last Chance.

While not the biggest saloon in Independence it was one of the oldest, its name coming from the time when it was the last saloon this side of The Rockies. It could no longer make that claim but tradition had established it as the meeting place of those about to set off across the prairies. Colin, as he pushed open the swing doors, felt himself the centre of attention as men, pausing in their conversation, glanced towards the stranger. Their attention was momentary. they had merely looked to see if the newcomer was someone they knew. Colin eased through the throng and leaned against the bar.

'Whiskey.'

'Sure.' The bartender put a bottle and glass on the counter. 'You a stranger in town?'

'That's right.' Colin filled the glass. 'Know a man named Mark Longdon?'

'Mr Longdon?' The bartender nodded. 'He's over in the corner, the man in the plug hat talking to the prospector.'

Colin nodded his thanks, paid for his drink and, carrying the glass, walked over to where Longdon sat in conversation. He waited until the prospector had left and sat in the vacant seat.

'I hear you're heading west,' he said shortly. 'Is that right?'

'I have organized a party to make the journey,' admitted Longdon. He was a tall, dandified looking man with an ornate waistcoat and good broadcloth. Outwardly he seemed the last man to attempt the journey but Colin was not fooled by appearances. It took money to outfit a wagon and Longdon obviously had money. Equally obviously he was a man of strength and character; if he wasn't he would never be contemplating the trip at all.

'I'd like to hire out to you if you need any help,' said Colin. 'The livery stable attendant told me you might be looking for a couple of men.'

'I was,' said Longdon regretfully. 'But I'm full up. I wanted a hunter and scout and now have both.' He hesitated. 'If it was just passage you wanted I could fit you in. You could act as general handler, keeping track of the cows, helping with the oxen, things like that. I couldn't pay you though.'

'Thanks for the offer,' said Colin sincerely. 'But I was looking for something better than that.' He sipped at his drink. 'You know of anyone else who might be interested?'

'Looking for a wagon boss, you mean?'

'No. Looking for a hunter or scout. I've done both.'

Longdon nodded, his eyes drifting over the young man. Colin wore the clothes he had purchased while in Texas, and his high-heeled boots, low slung holsters and leather jacket gave him the appearance of a cowpuncher. Longdon stared at the twin Colts hanging low from their cartridge belts.

'You look like a cowpuncher to me.'

'I worked a spell down in the cow country.' Colin dismissed the objection. 'Well?'

'Sam Curtway was looking for a man,' said Longdon. He hesitated. 'I don't want you to misunderstand me but I don't want to steer you wrong. Sam's a nice man but his train isn't as good as it could be. Still, you can find that out for yourself. You'll find him down at the assembly ground if you're interested.'

'I'm interested,' said Colin. He finished his drink. 'And thanks.'

The assembly ground was at the western edge of town and was just what its name implied. Here assembled the wagons readying for the Californian journey, checking and examining their equipment and gear for the final time before taking the trail across the prairie. Cooking fires sent thin columns of smoke towards the sky and children were everywhere, running between the wagons, playing hide and seek, racing and enjoying the excitement preceding the journey.

Sam Curtway was a man past middle age, a short, stocky, red-faced man with a thick crop of red hair and a shrewd pair of light blue eyes. He stared hard at Colin.

'So Longdon sent you, did he?'

'He told me you might be in need of a man.' Colin rested his shoulders against a wagon and returned the other man's stare. 'He also said that your train wasn't as good as it could be.'

'Longdon talks too much,' said Curtway without anger. 'But he was right.' He seemed to arrive at a decision. 'Come and have a bite to eat while we talk about it.' He led the way between the wagons to where a plump, comfortable woman stooped over a pot suspended over a fire. 'Mary, we got a guest.'

'Pleased to meet you.' The plump woman bobbed her head. 'Julia!' she shouted suddenly. 'Julia, come and get it.'

'Coming, Ma.' A tall girl jumped from a wagon and came towards the fire, halting as she saw Colin. For a moment they stared at each other then she blushed and sat down, smoothing her skirt over her knees.

'This is Colin Bowman,' said Curtway. 'Colin, meet my daughter, Julia.'

They nodded to each other, each liking what they saw. Julia took after her father in that she had red hair and was barely out of her teens. While not startlingly beautiful she had a certain attractiveness and Colin, who had roamed far and was still alone, wondered how it was that she was still unmarried. She noticed his gaze and busied herself with the cooking pot, making a brave show of her ringless hand.

Sam answered Colin's unasked question.

'Julia was fit to get married but her man got himself killed by a horse.' He spooned beans and belly pork into his mouth. 'You married, Colin?'

'No.'

'No wagon then?'

'Just a horse.' Colin ate for a while in silence; the questions, he knew, were in order that Sam could size him up. He had no objection to that, only a fool would take on a complete stranger without satisfying himself that the man was reliable before starting such a proposed journey and Colin, for his own part, had no wish to travel with a fool.

Sam finished his food without resuming his questions, accepted a tin cup of coffee from his wife, lit a pipe and made himself comfortable.

'So you want to ride with us,' he said abruptly. 'What's on your mind?'

'Hunter, scout, driver, I can make myself useful.' Colin smiled at Mary as she handed him coffee. 'How many in your party?'

'A dozen wagons.' Sam hesitated. 'Look, Colin, you look a right man and I'll square with you. Longdon, damn him, was right in what he said. Money's short on this party and we're cutting things fine. Do you know the trail?'

'No.'

'You're honest at any rate.' Sam was disappointed. 'I was hoping to get a wagon boss who knew the trail.'

'Why?' Colin stared at the red-headed man. 'For that you'll have to pay up to maybe a thousand dollars. Hell, the trail's well-marked by now, anyone could follow it. I . . . ' He broke off, staring at Curtway. 'You are going to take the old trail, aren't you?'

'I was thinking that maybe it wouldn't be such a good idea.' Curtway explained further. 'We're farming folk and what we want is good land. We ain't that interested in gold. I heard tell that there was good soil down in the Nations and I was figuring to stake out a section and put in some crops.'

'I see.' Colin sipped at his coffee. 'You know what you're doing?'

'I know.' Curtway drew at his pipe. 'I ain't a youngster, Colin, but I've got sense. Everyone who can build a wagon, buy a horse or hitch a ride is heading for the goldfields. So some of them will find gold but a lot of them won't. I'm not a gambling man, never have been, and I'm not a miner either. Gold or no gold men have got to eat and a man with a full stomach and no gold is better off than a man who owns a mine and who hasn't food. I put my trust in the soil. Food, Colin, food and houses and a decent community, that's what we're after. Out there, maybe we can find it.'

'Homesteaders.' Colin stared into the fire, his memory playing with the contempt the cattle barons had shown for those who had entered the range and built their homes. There had been ugly incidents, burnings, cattle driven over ripe crops and even a couple of shootings.

'You can call us that,' agreed Sam. 'Don't you like the idea?'

'No harm in it, I suppose. It all depends where you aim to settle.'

'I told you, in the Nations. No one

owns that land and it's good land.' Sam looked at the young man. 'I guess that you wouldn't want to stay with us now that you know that we ain't going to California.'

Colin shrugged, not answering.

'Not that we could pay you much,' said Sam. 'I told you, money's short between us.'

Colin rose to his feet and hitched up the guns around his waist.

'Let's take a look at the wagons,' he said.

'You still interested?' Sam jumped to his feet, his eagerness betraying his need for a man who knew something of the country into which they intended to go. Colin realized why when he inspected the train.

It consisted of a dozen wagons in all shapes of repair. Mostly they were modelled after the great Connestogas with their high bodies and five-foot wheels, their canvas covers and their teams of oxen. But there the resemblance ended. These wagons looked

121

what they were, farm wagons hastily adapted, overloaded for the most part and looking unsafe. Colin realized what Longdon had meant when he said that the train wasn't as good as it could be.

Sam read the expression on the young man's face.

'They ain't too good,' he admitted, 'but it's the best we have. We'll make out.'

'You think so?' Colin shrugged. 'Once you hit rough country your trip will be over. Hell man, you're not giving yourself a chance.' He walked around the wagons, inspecting their structure, examining the animals and looking at the faces of the men and women who lived in or around the wagons. When he returned to the fire his face was thoughtful.

'Look, Sam,' he said abruptly. 'I'll speak straight. When do you aim to start?'

'As soon as we can find a scout and guide.'

'How many men have turned down

the job?' Colin shrugged. 'Never mind, I can guess the answer. No one will take the job, am I right?'

'Not without more money than we can afford to pay,' admitted Curtway.

'So you're stuck here,' said Colin. 'Your money is running out and soon you'll have to either move or sell out. If you move you'll get to the first patch of hard going and then you'll break down.'

'We can settle wherever we stop.'

'Can you?' Colin looked doubtful. 'Maybe you won't be given the chance.'

'Indians?' Sam caught the meaning. 'They won't touch us.'

'I wouldn't gamble on it,' said Colin dryly. 'If you'll take my advice you won't settle in the Nations at all, you'll go right through into New Mexico and Arizona. From there you can get into Southern California.'

'You think that's best?'

'I don't know,' admitted Colin. 'If you want land you should be able to find it without going so far.' He came to a decision. 'You want me to be boss?'

For a moment Sam hesitated. He had hoped to be wagon boss himself but that hope had died as the weary weeks had dragged past. He was a farmer, he admitted it, and already he had had trouble keeping the train together. If he was to get moving at all it had to be soon. He nodded.

'All right. We'll do as you say.'

'Then call a meeting.' Colin rose to his feet. 'I want every man to be ordered to unload his wagon down to safe limits. Carry only what you need, tools, seeds, medical supplies. Sell all the rest.'

'How about food?'

'What are you carrying?'

'A hundred pounds of flour and fifty pounds of bacon a head.'

'Too much.' Colin was impatient. 'Cut the flour by half and the bacon down to twenty pounds a wagon. Sell the rest. How are you off for guns?'

'Most men have a rifle, some a shotgun too.'

'Pistols, horses, spare oxen?' Colin

shook his head at the other's expression. 'We'd better get busy. We've got a lot to do before we can roll.'

It was an understatement. The wagons had been assembling too long and things had got out of hand. Colin and Sam went from wagon to wagon and at each their orders were the same.

'Unload. Check the wagons and only put back the things you can't do without. Cut down on food but take plenty of water barrels. Check your guns. Each man to have a pistol and rifle. Check your horses, cows, and oxen.'

There were grumbles but Colin dealt with them firmly.

'You do it or you stay behind. We roll at dawn and those who aren't ready won't be allowed to come.'

It was hard, but it was necessary. Colin knew that the speed of the train would be dictated by the slowest wagon and breakdowns could slow them almost to a crawl. Later, while the wagons hummed with activity, Colin explained what he had in mind.

'I'm a hunter and can supply you with food. I can scout too and find a trail. The thing to do is to get near a fort as soon as possible. That way you can settle without worrying too much about Indians. But you must have guns to beat off attacks, spare oxen and horses to replace losses and light wagons so as to make speed. The Nations is unexplored territory and we want to be ready for anything.'

He touched on more personal matters.

'How are you going to pay me?'

'We've got some money,' said Sam. 'How much do you want?'

'A thousand dollars. For that I'll guide you and supply meat to the entire train. You pay me when you finally settle providing that you settle at the first good, protected place. Agreed?'

'A thousand dollars.' Sam rubbed at his chin. 'It's a lot of money.'

'You can claim the money received from the sale of the extra food and other junk these people are carrying.' Colin rose to his feet. 'I'm not arguing. Either you accept the offer or you don't.' He looked down at the red-headed man. 'Well?'

Curtway nodded.

7

In 1867 Indian Territory, or the Nations as it was popularly called, was largely unsurveyed prairie and as yet unexplored wilderness. Within certain defined boundaries were tribes of Indians who had been given that area as their own. But no one quite knew just where the Indian Territory began and Indians roamed from the Red River to the Arkansas, their only restraint being a small cavalry attached to one of the scattered forts. These detachments were supposed to maintain law and order, protect the white man and enforce peace on the Indians. They failed because they could do nothing else.

The white men themselves did not help matters. Word and rumour had spread that the Indian Territory contained great riches in minerals, soil and gold. The State of Texas had already claimed a slice of the Nations and was ready to fight for it. Kansas, New Mexico, and Colorado were eager to follow the example of the Lone Star State and had sent small parties of surveyors into the Nations in an effort to both map the territory and to gain some idea of the wealth contained within it.

The Indians, Seminoles, Choctaws, Chickasaws and their tribal brothers the Sioux had resisted such excursions and the scalps of many white men hung from the coup poles of the lodges. The neighbouring states resented this rough justice and demanded that the cavalry afford a greater degree of protection. The Indian Office in charge of Indian Affairs replied with the accusation that any white men entering the Nations were doing so at their own risk and must accept responsibility. The Indians, convinced that they were in the right, unrestrained or angered by the cavalry, took reprisals wherever and whenever they could. In short the Indian Territory was a simmering cauldron of violence with murder, torture and sudden death waiting for anyone fool enough to enter into it without taking full precautions.

Into this area Colin led his train of twelve ill-equipped wagons.

He was uneasy, alert, ready for any trouble which might come, but as he rode his horse he seemed wholly at ease. At first the journey had been without incident, his insistence on lightening the loads had enabled the oxen to haul the wagons without strain to themselves or the vehicles. So the spirits of the wagon folk rose, as day followed day and Independence fell far behind.

'Colin!'

He turned at the call and reined in as Julia rode up beside him. Now that they had left civilization she had donned a pair of her father's jeans, a garb which would have earned her hoots of derision in any town, and rode her horse with an ease which betrayed her skill in the saddle.

'Hello Julia, your Pa know where you are?'

'Of course.' She guided her horse beside his own. 'Ma didn't like it but then Ma's old fashioned. What's the harm in me riding out with you on a hunt?'

'Plenty.' Colin knew the strict code of the West as applied to women-folk. 'You want folk to talk?'

'What about?'

'For an intelligent girl you can talk mighty dumb,' said Colin brutally. 'If you had a husband back in the train you wouldn't be so free.'

'Well I haven't, nor sweetheart either.' From her expression Colin knew that she had been spoiled. 'You hunting again today?'

'No.'

'Why not?'

'We've got meat and to spare. There's no sense in killing for the sake of it.'

'There's plenty of game.'

'Sure there is.' He turned in the saddle to stare at her. 'But for how long? We're among the first to come this way but we won't be the last. If we kill everything we see just for the fun of it what are other trains going to eat?'

'Do you always think of others?'

'Most times, why, don't you?'

'I don't know.' She rode in silence for a while. 'Were you in the war Colin?'

'I was.'

'North or South?'

'I chose the winning side,' he said without emotion. He lifted himself in his stirrups and stared towards the horizon. For a while he stared ahead and then sat back again. 'Why do you ask?'

'Just curious.' She picked at her reins. 'Matt, that was the man I was supposed to marry, he fought for the Union.' She gave a little laugh. 'He was a lot older than I am but everyone took it for granted that we would get hitched as soon as the war was over. Then it was over and Matt didn't come back. We heard after that he'd got himself kicked in the head by a horse.'

'So?'

'So I wasn't so upset as I should have been. In fact I wasn't upset at all.' She looked at him from the corner of her eyes. 'You got a girl, Colin?'

For answer he turned and stared at her, reading in her eyes the same thing he had seen in Nancy's so long ago now. It was the wedding fever. Women were scarce in the West and didn't lack suitors. Men were eager to marry and raise a family and the few available women were soon snapped up. But it went deeper than that. A single woman was an unprotected woman. A single man was a footloose man.

'What's on your mind, Julia?' He was abrupt, so abrupt that the blood flushed her cheeks.

'Nothing.'

'Yes there is. You hanker for a husband or what?'

'If I did it wouldn't be you,' she

133

snapped. 'Some people are too conceited for their own good.'

'And some women forget how to be womanlike,' he said pointedly. 'When you start wearing pants, Julia, then you must expect to be treated as a man. You can't have it both ways.' He craned himself in the saddle again and her curiosity mastered her anger.

'What you see, Colin?'

'Nothing.'

'Are you sure?' Her doubt was obvious.

'You heard what I said.' Inexperience made his words rougher than he intended. He lacked the knowledge of how to handle a woman with soft words and compliments. He felt the lack and compensated for it by a curt manner towards the fair sex. An older, more mature, woman would have recognized his manner for what it was, a cover for his shyness, but Julia thought that he was just being rude.

'If you don't know what it is then maybe I can find out.' She touched spurs to the flanks of her mount and, before he could stop her, had darted from his side. He followed immediately but before the horses had covered a furlong knew that he was in for a long hard chase.

Julia's mount was fresh, she was light and the animal was eager to stretch its legs. Colin's horse was tired and had to carry the heavier weight of his rider together with his equipment. Even so it would only be a matter of time before he ran her down. He did his best to shorten the period.

He had lied to the girl. He had seen a plume of dust far ahead, dust which could mean nothing more than a herd of buffalo crossing the prairie or a group of wild horses. But equally so it could mean that a party of riders were in that direction and, in the Nations, such a party could consist only of cavalry or Indians. But cavalry would have left a longer, more regular trail.

'Julia!' He called then, as it became apparent that she had no intention of stopping, dug in his spurs and raced after her. As he rode he loosened the Winchester in its scabbard and the twin Colts in their holsters at his belt. His shotgun he had left back at the wagons.

'Julia!' He thinned his lips as a flock of wild turkeys suddenly exploded from the grass to his right. Immediately he snatched out his left hand Colt and thumbed back the hammer. The weapon exploded in a rolling sound of thunder as he thumbed the gun with his left hand, sending lead whining towards the place where the turkeys had risen. Julia, startled by the shots, reined and turned.

'Colin! What's wrong?'

'After me, hurry!' Savagely he whipped her mount and set it lunging back the way it had come. Holstering his empty pistol he drew its twin and, crouching low over the neck of his horse, raced after the girl. Behind him came a peculiar thrumming sound and his horse whinneyed as to sudden pain.

'Colin!' Julia had regained control of

her horse and had reined within sight of the wagon train. 'What's the matter with you? Why did you whip my horse?'

'Indians.' He gestured behind him. 'You were riding right into them.'

'Indians!' For a moment she betrayed her fear of the lurking danger, then laughed. 'You must think I'm a child! Was that the only way you could win the race?'

'I wasn't racing,' he said evenly. 'And the next time you do a thing like that I'll shoot the horse from under you.'

'So you weren't racing.' Her contempt was plain. 'So you just can't stand to be beaten by a woman, is that it?'

'You can think that if you want to.'

'I do want to, you leave me no option.' Her contempt deepened. 'Indians! A poor excuse.'

'Was it?' Colin turned so that she could see the back of his saddle. Reaching down he gripped the slender shaft of wood which had pierced the leather and injured the horse. Savagely he tugged it out and held it on his palm. 'So there were no Indians. Then where did this come from?'

Julia turned pale and swayed as she stared at the painted wood and feathers of the Indian arrow.

Later, back at the wagon train, Colin called Sam to one side and talked about it.

'They know we're here,' he said. 'It was probably a hunting party Julia ran into, there are no barbs on the arrow so it's my guess we bumped into some hunters. But they'll take back word to their lodges and we can expect a war party to come after us.'

'You sure about that Colin?'

'No, I'm not sure. There's a lot I don't know about Indians so it's anyone's guess as to what will happen. But we are in the Indian Territory and they aren't going to like it. We wouldn't be the first wagon train that's been attacked and I don't suppose that we'll be the last. The thing is to keep alert and beat them off if they try anything.'

'A pity,' said Sam. 'Everything was running so smooth up to now, just like going on a picnic. Now this has to happen.' He looked at Colin. 'How bad do you think it is?'

'It'll be bad,' said the young man. 'Even a little will be too much.' He glanced back at the wagons. 'How are they likely to act?'

'They're good folk,' said Sam. 'Farming folk but they can fight if they have to.'

'They may have to.' Colin stood up on the front of the wagon. He had mounted beside Sam on his return and, from the body of the wagon he could hear Mary fuss over her daughter. Julia had been shaken by the turn of events. What had started out to be an innocent ride with some pleasant teasing of the young scout had almost turned into tragedy.

It was late afternoon, the sun falling towards the west and almost directly before them. The prairie rolled on either side merging with a range of low hills to the north and covered with brushwood before them. To the south it ran down to the Red River still a long way away. Colin had set his course so as to cross Arkansas and head to the Canadian river further west. By running almost alongside the river beyond the northern hills he hoped to remain in country well-stocked with game. The game, obviously, had also attracted the Indians.

'When do we camp, Colin?' Sam was uneasy. He repeatedly turned his head from side to side and his hand was never far from the butt of the Colt at his waist.

'Give it a little longer. We can get plenty of wood further on and I want to hear what the outriders have to report.'

'Maybe they've run into trouble?' Sam was pessimistic. The train had two outriders to whom Colin had given strict instructions to report back the moment they noticed anything poten-tially dangerous. They were family men and he guessed that they wouldn't disobey. The thought of danger would send them back to protect their families.

'I doubt it.' Colin shaded his eyes. 'Here they come. They're riding slow and easy. so I guess they didn't see anything.' He pointed forward. 'We'll camp by that clump of trees. Place the wagons in a circle around the entire clump, you know what to do.' He whistled to his horse, mounting from the moving wagon. 'I'll take a short scout that way just to be sure the Indians aren't lying in ambush. See you.'

Sam lifted his hand as the young man rode off and then sent his whip cracking over the heads of the lead oxen. They lowed, leaning into their yokes and, slowly, the clump of trees came closer.

Colin rejoined the farmer as the wagons broke rank and moved to circle the clump of trees. He sat his horse, waiting until the oxen had been unyoked, the wagons drawn close and the cattle driven into the inner area. He called to Sam.

'Better have some of the men go with the youngsters to collect wood, and collect plenty of it. Fill up with water too. Then get the evening meal cooked and relieve the guards on the oxen.'

The oxen, unlike the domestic animals and horses, were left on the prairie so that they could eat their fill of the succulent buffalo grass. Guards watched over them though usually the chore was detailed to a couple of men. Now Colin insisted on trebling the night-guards.

'Four to watch the oxen and two to keep awake in camp,' he ordered. 'Change watch every four hours. Arrange it among yourselves.'

'Is that necessary, Colin?' Sam rubbed at his chin. 'That means that every man in camp will have to stand a turn at guard. They may not like it.'

'Then they can lump it.' Colin was irritable with fatigue and the sense of approaching danger. 'See that every man is armed or sleeps with his guns.' He saw the farmer's expression. 'So you think I'm taking unnecessary precautions, is that it?'

'We ain't seen nothing,' said Sam.

'What did you expect to see, the Indians come out in full view so that you can shoot at them?' Colin shook his head. 'This is getting us nowhere. I know the men are tired and that they need their rest, but we can't afford to take things easy. Now let's eat before we start drawing on one another.'

He meant it as a joke but it went deeper than that. Tired men are apt to argue and, when they have weapons at their belts, sometimes the arguments tended to become violent and permanent. Colin was glad when Mary announced that the evening meal was ready.

Colin had insisted that the wagon train eat only twice a day, at morning before starting and at evening when making camp. The noon halt was mainly to change the oxen and to rest the beasts, the men snatching a cup of coffee and a hunk of bread or chewing at a piece of cooked meat as they rode. His reasons, as he had told Sam, were simple.

'Oxen are slow, it's a good wagon train that can make fifteen miles a day. The longer we are on the road, the worse we'll be when we arrive, and anyway, you don't want to arrive too late. You've got to get a crop in as soon as you can or rely on local game to keep you for almost a year. Maybe you can do it, but the winters can be bad in the Territory. Let's not waste any more time than we have to.'

He had made sense, and the wagoners, even while they grumbled at the pace set by the young man, had to admit he was right. They had wasted too much time in Independence and, farmers all, they itched to break new ground, get in their seed and erect cabins against the winter. Unlike most parties travelling West they had no real objective. They would not be able to rely on earlier settlers being able to provide them with food and shelter during the winter. They would stand or fall by their own efforts.

The evening meal was the big social occasion of the day. Then, for the first time, the party relaxed. Fires blazed before most wagons and the big fire in the centre was kept going all night ready to start breakfast at the first crack of dawn. Colin's success as a hunter had kept the party well supplied so that there was plenty of fresh meat for all. Coffee was still plentiful and while sugar was scarce they had milk from the domestic cows which were hitched to the back of the wagons.

Once the meal was over, the dishes washed and stacked away, the smaller fires doused and the younger children put to bed, the elders and older children relaxed. Then it was that stories would be swapped, sometimes of the war but mostly of things rumoured rather than actually known. The adolescents would try to act grown up, the oldsters would sit and smoke and stare into the fire as they built dreams of the new life to come. And, at times, there would be music and dancing, the couples swaying in the square dance to the tune of a fiddle.

To Sam's surprise Colin made no objection when the fiddler struck up a tune.

'Ain't you thinking that it might be better if we kept quiet?' he asked. 'Sound travels a long way at night.'

'Let them enjoy themselves,' said Colin. 'The Indians know we're here so it won't make any difference as far as they are concerned. But it will make a difference to us. Let them forget Indians and danger and hardship while they can.'

'Just so's you know what you're doing.' Sam relit his pipe. 'Makes a mighty pretty scene, though, don't it?'

'Promise of things to come,' said Colin. He rose to his feet as Julia came towards where he and Sam sat. She had changed her clothes and now wore feminine gingham. She had brushed her hair until it shone like burnished copper and had tied it back with a green ribbon. Her face was flushed from excitement and, in the firelight, she looked very beautiful.

'Care to give a girl a dance, Colin?'

'Sorry, Julia,' he said with real regret. 'I guess I never learned the way how.'

'I'll teach you.' Julia extended her arms in invitation. 'It's simple, really, and good fun.'

'No thanks.'

'You don't want to dance with me?'

'I don't want to dance with anyone, not tonight.'

'I see.' She bit her lip, her face registering her disappointment, then, as a big, hulking young farmer approached her, turned to him with a smile. 'Lem will dance with me, won't you, Lem?'

'Sure will,' he grinned. 'Let's go.'

Sam watched them, then glanced at Colin.

'Seems to me that a man should relax sometimes,' he said. 'If he don't then he gets all hard and bitter inside.'

'Meaning me?'

'Meaning that all work and no play isn't good for anyone.' Sam hesitated. 'I'm a lot older than you are, Colin, and I guess I look on you as a son. I never did have a boy, only Julia, and I kinda miss having a son. I wouldn't like to see any boy of mine get so that he couldn't enjoy himself.'

'I'll make out.'

'Sure you will, but for how long? A man's got to let himself laugh at times, Colin. He's got to mix with other folk and take an interest in them. If he don't then he gets so that he can't.'

'So you told me.' Colin had no intention of arguing about it.

From his holsters he lifted his twin Colts, set one before him and broke open the other. He examined the cartridges, tested the firing pin and reloaded the weapon before turning his attention to the other. Satisfied, he slipped the guns back into their holsters, hitching the belts around his slender waist until the butts came readily to hand. He looked up and caught Sam's expression.

'You figure on trouble, Colin?'

'In Indian Territory only a fool would ever figure on anything else.' Colin glanced up towards the sky. 'It's getting late. Better tell the folk to quit their dancing and get some rest. Detail the guards and tell them to keep watch.'

'What you aim to do?'

'I'm taking a ride. Maybe I'll find Indian sign, maybe not.'

'Or maybe you'll collect an arrow in the dark. Why don't you stay in camp? You look all tuckered out and you need rest more than any of us.'

'I won't be long,' said Colin. 'I'll whistle when I return so tell the guards to hold their fire if they hear me.' He touched the brim of his hat in farewell and went to find his horse.

He rode for an hour, circling the camp, eyes and ears alert for any sound or sight of danger. He knew that he would not find any Indians but he hoped that, if they were assembling for an attack, he would gain some clue as to their whereabouts and numbers. He found nothing and rode back to camp, his eyes burning with fatigue and his body stiff from almost continuous riding. The guards passed him at his whistle and he bedded down by the central fire.

Despite his tiredness it was a long time before he fell asleep. The night had suddenly grown very quiet, and, aside from the occasional howl of a coyote, nothing disturbed the stillness. Straining his ears Colin could just make out the low conversation of the men guarding the oxen and, from time to time, one of the camp guards would walk beside the wagons, his eyes searching the darkness beyond the light of the central fire.

Everything seemed as safe and as secure as he could make it. Any attack would be spotted and warning given in good time.

Colin finally slept, a light, dream-haunted sleep in which he again re-lived that night of terror when the Sioux had burned his family and their home. He rode again with Uncle Zeke and sat in lonely vigil beside the dying man. He tasted the terror of imminent death as he clung beneath the bridge, writhed to the remembered torture of crude surgery and woke, sweating, in the first pale light of dawn.

He relaxed after a quick look round. Everything was normal, the Indians, apparently, had not attacked. For a while he lay in his blankets, and then, shivering from the pre-dawn cold, rose and laved his face and hands. One of the guards smiled and called a greeting.

'Up early, Colin.'

'I couldn't sleep.' Colin joined the man and stared from the camp into the pearly mist covering the prairie. 'Have a quiet night?'

'Sure, not a sound or a cry. I guess the Indians knew better than to try anything.'

Colin nodded, still not wholly at ease, then dismissed his thoughts as he set about preparing morning coffee. Within a short while the camp was awake, everyone laughing at their previous fears, but when the mist finally lifted they discovered that they were not as fortunate as they thought.

Eighteen oxen were lying dead on the prairie.

8

They lay where they had fallen, the great beasts sprawled limp and lifeless on the grass. Colin stared down at them, his eyes narrowed as he sought for tracks, then he turned to Sam.

'Who was on guard detail during the last watch?'

'Lem Shaw, Brad Murphy, Mike Langthorne and Abe Hyam.'

'Bring them here.' Colin waited until the men had grouped before him. 'Can you account for this?' He gestured towards the dead beasts.

'We didn't hear a thing.' Lem Shaw, the big youngster with whom Julia had danced the previous night, shuffled his feet as he answered. 'The Indians must have sneaked up on their bellies and did the job.'

'Sure they did.' Colin stared again at a dead animal. 'They crept up and knifed them, but the oxen must have made a noise if the Indians didn't. You mean to say that you didn't hear them lowing?'

'We heard that,' said Abe Hyam. 'But beasts always make a noise just before dawn.'

'That sort of noise?' Colin restrained his anger. 'How were you stationed?' He looked at their faces. 'All right, I can guess. Instead of scattering around the beasts you all clung together. Maybe you did some smoking and it's certain that you did plenty of talking. When the mists grew thick you got scared and didn't bother to find out what was making the animals cry out. Damn you!'

'Watch yourself,' said Lem. 'I don't aim to be spoken to like that.'

'You fell down on the job,' said Colin. He made an effort to restrain his anger. 'A team and a half of oxen slaughtered under your very noses. Well, as you had the job of guarding them you lose the beasts.'

'Like hell we do!' Mike Langthorne glowered at the young man. 'My animals ain't been touched, why should I lose them?'

'Listen!' Colin raised his voice. 'We started as a unit and we're going to stay that way. Those oxen have to be made up one way or another. You had the job of guarding them and yet they were killed without you as much as firing a shot to scare off the Indians. You've all got spare oxen; well, you'll lose those animals so that the loss will be made good. Now quit arguing, hitch up, and let's get rolling.'

'No one touches my oxen,' said Langthorne. He stepped forward. 'So it's tough luck that someone's lost their animals, but that's their hard luck, not mine. I've got a full team and spares and I'm hanging on to them.'

'The four of you will replace the oxen lost,' said Colin. 'At least you'll do it this way. You'll each find three oxen to give to those who've lost their beasts.'

'I've lost a couple,' said Brad

Murphy. 'How do I stand?'

'You chip in one more.' Colin suddenly lost his patience. 'Hell, I'm not arguing about it. These wagons have got to roll and we need oxen to get them moving. You think that I'll leave a wagon behind so as you can nurse your animals?' His words made sense, especially to those who had lost their animals. Without oxen the wagons would be stranded and it was only justice that the men who had the task of guarding the animals should help to meet the loss. Even at that Colin was being more than fair in only asking them to replace two-thirds of the dead animals.

'I'll lend oxen,' said Langthorne. 'But I won't give them. I'll be needing them when we settle.'

'You'll give them.' Colin stared the man in the eyes. 'Now break out three of your beasts and look sharp about it.'

'I won't.' Langthorne was stubborn. 'Damn it, who are you to give away my stock?'

'I'm the boss of this train,' said Colin evenly. 'While I'm the boss you do as I say.' His voice softened. 'You aim to argue about it?'

It was an invitation. Langthorne knew it and knew too that he must meet it or back down. Men, in the West, made their own law and disputes were settled in the smoke of roaring Colts. For a moment the farmer hesitated, then, the thought of losing his animals decided him. He grabbed at the pistol at his waist.

As a draw it was so slow as to be almost ludicrous. The farmer had signalled his intention and, even as his hand gripped the butt of his pistol, Colin acted. His arm moved in a practised motion, light glimmered from the barrel of his Colt and the sharp explosion echoed around the camp. Langthorne, looking suddenly stupid, stared down at the blood-filled welt across the back of his right wrist.

'Satisfied?' Colin poised his heavy pistol. 'Or would you like to try again?'

'I . . . ' Langthorne gulped, knowing that the young man could have sent his bullet into his heart as easily as merely creasing his hand. For a moment he hesitated, then, as he saw the unsympathetic faces turned towards him, backed down. 'I'm satisfied.'

'Good. Now get that hand tied up and let's roll.'

The men dissolved into a blur of well-ordered activity.

All that day the wagons moved across the prairie while behind them the buzzards swooped in the sky over the dead oxen. Sam, staring back at the wheeling shapes, shuddered and turned to Colin.

'Think they'll do the same again?'

'I don't know.' Colin had ridden far that morning and had returned to snatch a cup of coffee and hunk of bread before riding out again. 'Tonight we'll corral the oxen within the wagons, they can be taken out to feed until late dark. But that won't be good enough. We'll either have to let them feed during the day or take a chance at night.'

'And then the Indians can get at them again.' Sam shook his head. 'It beats me why they do it. I always thought that they'd ride right against us.'

'The Sioux would, but not the Chickasaws. They don't fight that way. Mostly they steal things, shoot arrows into the oxen and wear the train down. If they kill enough oxen and horses we'll have to abandon the wagons and proceed on foot. Then we'll be easy meat to a war-party.'

'Maybe they'll leave us alone now.' Sam was trying to be optimistic. 'You think that they might, Colin? Couldn't we buy them off, give them gifts, things like that?'

'I doubt it. Twenty years ago, yes, but not now. The Indians are fighting for survival and they know it. They've got new chiefs and have learned from the white man. Traders have sold them repeating rifles and the Indians have learned to fight as a group. Back at Independence I talked to a couple of soldiers from New Mexico and they told me that the Apaches have managed to unite themselves. Up north Chief Sitting Bull is bringing the Dakotas, the Cheyenne and the Sioux together. Down this way the Sioux are trying to organize the local tribes. They may not do it but they are teaching them a new method of fighting.'

'They can't beat the white man,' said Sam. 'They'll never do that.'

'I agree, but the Indians don't know what we know. The Indians are concerned only with the white men in their lands. They hate the reservations and want to reclaim their own land. They see wagon trains, prospectors, traders, surveyors, all manner of people pressing in and taking what is theirs and they don't like it. Sure, they can never win in any war, we know that. But knowing it won't help us any if they attack. We'll be dead.'

'Nice prospect,' said Sam. He looked

around at the prairie, now yielding to wooded slopes. 'Good land for farming, this. If it wasn't for the Indians I'd feel like settling down right here.'

'Wait until we reach the fort.' Colin stood up on the wagon seat and stared towards the north. 'You'll be safer there.'

'If we get there,' said Sam. He looked back at the train, at the outriders well to either side, and at the small herd of cows following on behind guarded and driven by just a couple of boys. 'Langthorne's holding a grudge against you, Colin. He's talking about holding a meeting tonight to displace you.'

'So?'

'So some of the folk may side with him. You've driven them pretty hard one way and another and they don't like the idea of the guards having to make up the lost animals. They didn't like the way you made Langthorne go for his gun either. They say that you're a gunman and too bossy. Thought I'd let you know.'

'It doesn't bother me,' said Colin. 'If they want to kick me out then I'll go. But I want paying before I leave.'

'Langthorne doesn't know what he's talking about,' said Sam. 'He figures on himself being elected wagon boss but he just hasn't got what it takes. The first time we're attacked he'll go all to pieces.' Sam thoughtfully cracked his whip above the heads of his lead oxen. 'How far to the nearest fort, Colin?'

'Not too far. Why?'

'We could head for it, settle there and then you'd be paid. Once these people get their fingers into dirt they'll forget all about the past. You could stake out a section for yourself and settle down with us. Get married, maybe.' Sam glanced sidewise at the young man. 'A man ought to get married while he's still young enough to enjoy it.'

'I'll think about it.' Colin had his thoughts elsewhere. Again he climbed on the wagon seat and stared towards the north. Sam looked up at him.

'See anything?'

'Come and look.'

'Look where?' Sam dropped the reins and climbed up beside the young man. He shaded his eyes and peered towards the north.

'See it?' Colin pointed. 'Just above that peak. See?'

'See what? I . . . ' Sam broke off as his eyes focused on the distant peak. From it, rising like a thin trail into the sky, something billowed and wavered, plumed and shook before climbing steadily again into the heavens. 'Smoke!'

'Yes.' Colin was grim. 'Smoke signals. That means the Sioux are close to here.' He jumped down into the wagon. 'Keep this to yourself, no sense in alarming the others. But tell the outriders to keep the wagons close bunched and to be ready for anything. If anyone spots a war-party you know what to do.'

'Circle and fight.' Sam swallowed, his adam's apple bobbing in his throat. 'How far did you say that fort was?'

'With luck we'll be there tomorrow.'

'So close?' Sam grinned, then lost his smile. 'But if it's so near then . . . '

'That's right. If the Indians are going to attack they'll do it soon while we're still a distance from the fort.' Colin frowned thoughtfully at the distant column of smoke. 'How good are you on a horse, Sam?'

'Not so good, why?'

'I'd like to send a messenger to the fort to carry word that we're on our way and are liable to be attacked. With luck they will send out a column of cavalry to escort us in. If a messenger left now there's a good chance that the troops may arrive in time to prevent any attack at all. Sure you can't ride a horse?'

'No.' Sam was definite. 'And I ain't leaving my wagon either. We'll need every man and every gun if the Indians do attack. Why don't you go?'

'You've just told me,' said Colin. 'I'm a scout and I was a soldier. I'm used to warfare and I'll be needed.' He frowned at the lead oxen. 'How about Langthorne?'

'How about me?' Julia stepped from the body of the wagon and joined them on the front board.

'I heard what you said. Why can't I carry the message?'

'Are you crazy, girl! What about the Indians?' 'Well, what about them?' She turned from her father to Colin. 'I can handle a horse, you know that, and I can be spared. Just tell me how to reach the fort and I'll get going.'

Colin hesitated. What the girl said was true, she could handle a horse and could be spared. But he hesitated at sending her into an Indian-infested wilderness.

'Someone's got to go,' she reminded. 'And if the Indians are going to attack they won't worry about a lone messenger.' She smiled at Colin. 'Now stop arguing. Just tell me how to reach the fort.'

'Call Langthorne,' said Colin abruptly. 'And call Lem Shaw.'

'Why?'

'Three are better than one. You may

have to fight your way through and both men can handle guns good enough for Indians. Call them and let's get this thing started.'

Startled by the note of savagery in his voice she obeyed. Colin wasted little time when the three of them had reassembled.

'I want you to carry a message to Fort Holden,' he said. 'I've got a rough map and can give you rough directions. but that is all. You'll have to use your heads and eyes to find it, and everything you've got to avoid any Indians who may lie between the fort and us. You'll travel light and each take a couple of pistols and a shotgun. Ride together and keep moving. If you're attacked then shoot your way out.' Colin hesitated, looking at Julia.

'I can't ask you to take care of the girl, you'll have enough to do, but I'd take it kindly if you was to remember that she isn't a man.' He got down to business. 'All right, now here's the map, here's roughly where we are and here's where the fort should be. By cutting across this hill you could save time but don't do it. Stick to the open so as to avoid ambush. Don't gallop your horses too hard and be extra careful at night.' He folded the map and handed it to Julia. 'All right, you know what you have to do.'

The two men left to take their farewells of their families and to check their weapons and horses. Julia, changing into jeans, boots and leather jacket, looked like a young boy. She had tied up her hair and was wearing pistols low on her hips. She smiled at Colin's expression.

'Now don't tell me to ride in skirts, I can't do it. Anyway, I should dress like a man if I'm to do a man's work.'

'Be careful,' said Colin.

'I'll be careful,' she said. She smiled up at Sam, kissed her mother and, mounting her horse, joined Colin where he waited to ride out with the little party. 'How far are you coming with us?'

'Not far, just far enough to see that you get a good start.'

'The others will be here soon,' she said.

'So?' He looked surprised.

'You . . . ' She broke off as Langthorne and Shaw rode towards them. 'Let's go!'

Later, on his way back to the wagon train, Colin wondered at the expression in her eyes. He shrugged, annoyed with himself for his unexpected tenderness towards the red-haired girl, then forgot it in fresh worry.

Two more columns of smoke were lifting from the northern hills.

9

The camp was tense that night. Men spoke little, their eyes searching the blackness beyond the wagons, their hands nervously fingering pistols and rifles. The women too were quiet, scolding the children and sending them early to bed. Colin, tall and stern, walked around the camp, his eyes searching for faults.

'Get as many buckets filled from the water barrels as you can,' he ordered. 'Set them beside the wagons.'

Men hurried to obey, the events of the morning forgotten in the face of a greater danger. Colin might be bossy, stern and unrelenting, but he alone of them all knew what to do for the greatest safety.

The evening meal had been a hurried affair and as soon as it was over the camp readied for whatever might come.

All fires were doused but the central blaze, which was kept to a minimum. Within the circle of wagons the oxen and other livestock had been driven. Men armed with rifles sat at vantage points on the wagons, keeping, at Colin's insistence, below the canvas tops so that they would not be revealed by the firelight behind them. Other men, volunteers, lay in the grass just outside the camp, eyes and ears alert.

'Will they attack?' Sam asked the question for the dozenth time. Colin, his nerves rasped raw by the anxiety of the wagoners, controlled his impatience. Sam had a double worry. He was afraid for his wife and friends and he was afraid for his daughter.

'I don't know,' said Colin. 'I doubt if they'll attack in a full charge. Indians don't like to fight at night, but they may try sneaking up on us. The only thing we can do is to keep a close watch.'

'Yes.' Sam rubbed at his chin. 'I guess that's about all we can do at that. Watch and pray. You any good at praying, Colin?'

'No.'

'Me neither, but I guess I can find a few words.' He swallowed. 'It ain't so much me as I'm worried about, it's Julia. You reckon she'll be all right?'

'She's got two men with her and is well mounted. She'll get through.'

'You sure about that?'

'I'm sure,' said Colin and walked away. But he wasn't sure, he couldn't be sure. Suddenly he had a mental vision of Julia, impaled by an Indian arrow, sprawled lifeless on the prairie. The image sickened him and sent the hot blood pounding through his veins. But it was no anger, it was more like fear, the ghastly fear of not being able to prevent what might happen.

He tried to lose his fear in action.

Personally he went to every man, checking weapons, inspecting the water buckets and making certain that the children and women were under cover in the bodies of the wagons. For the men off-guard he had a few words of instruction and advice.

'Sleep easy until you're called. If anything happens then grab your guns and take a station under the wagon. Hold your fire until you see something to shoot at.' He ended with encouragement. 'I doubt as if they'll attack tonight. In any case men will be watching all night long, you don't have to worry about a thing.'

They smiled and voiced their thanks and went to rest with easy minds for the knowledge that someone who knew what he was doing was watching over them. To Sam, who could not sleep, Colin gave more detailed instructions.

'Let the men rest as much as they can. Change the outside guards and bring them in the moment it gets too dark to see anything.' He squinted up at the sky. 'Looks like cloud; if the starlight goes fetch them in anyway. Relieve the men on the wagons every hour, a tired man can't concentrate. Keep coffee and hot water boiling but don't let the men assemble around the fire. You can see a man for a mile when he's standing in front of a fire. Get the livestock and oxen settled if you can.'

'What do you aim to do, Colin?'

'I . . . ' Colin broke off as, on the other side of camp, a man screamed with sudden pain and fear. He rose from where he had sat on a wagon, twisting and turning as he crashed to the ground. Colin was beside him as soon as he had landed.

'Arrow.' The young man stared at the circle of heads staring towards him. 'Back to your positions! Remain behind cover. You!' He pushed at a too-curious man. 'Get under cover, you fool! You want to collect an arrow too?'

Something hissed from the darkness as he spoke and stuck quivering in the lead pole of a wagon. A second arrow followed the first and, within seconds, the air was full of the hissing shafts of death.

'They're sniping at us.' Colin scowled at the fire. 'I'd like to douse that but if we do then we'll be blinded. They know where we are, the light only helps them to find targets, but without the fire we can't see what is happening.' He stooped over the man who had been struck. The arrow had buried itself in his shoulder and blood made a thick, sticky mess down his side.

'How is he?' Sam, his face anxious, looked at the wound.

'Bad, but he could be worse.' Colin touched the arrow and the flesh around the wound. Gently his fingers probed into the flesh. The man groaned, his face drawn and sweating with agony.

'Take it easy,' he gasped. 'It's like a hot iron inside me.'

'We'll soon fix it.' Colin looked at Sam. 'Got any whiskey?'

'I got a jug, sure. You want it?'

'Yes.' Colin caught the farmer by the arm as he made to cross the camp. 'Not that way. Work around the wagons. You want to get hurt too?' Squatting down, Colin slipped his knife from its sheath and began to cut away the bloodsoaked clothing of the injured man. Sam returned with the whiskey and a can of hot water.

'Thanks.' Colin dipped a rag in the water and washed the blood away from the wound. 'The head of this arrow is barbed and we'll do more damage trying to pull it out than if we leave it alone.' His knife flashed as he cut the shaft a few inches above the wound. 'Cutting it out would be the answer but there's another way.' He picked up the jug and handed it to the injured man. 'Take a swig, a real good one.'

'Thanks.' The man drank and coughed. 'What you aim to do?'

'Just let's have another look.' Colin stooped over the man and, with a sudden violent movement, thrust the arrow completely through the shoulder so that the blood-stained head broke through the flesh on the other side.

The injured man writhed, a terrible groan escaping from his throat, then he relaxed as Colin showed him the arrow head. He had pulled the shaft completely through the wound.

'All over,' Colin said soothingly. 'Take another drink.'

'I need it.' The man was sweating and pale. He gulped at the raw spirit. 'Now what?'

'Now we fix it so that the wound won't rot.' Colin took the jug and, first washing the blood from the wound, deliberately poured the raw spirit on to the torn flesh.

The man screamed, his body heaving against the searing agony that tore at his shoulder, then slumped, half-fainting, as Colin bandaged the wound.

'Give him another drink, Sam,' snapped the young man. He smiled down at his victim. 'You're all right now. Favour that shoulder and it'll heal clean. But don't get yourself shot again, we ain't got that much whiskey.'

Despite his agony the man managed to raise a weak grin.

The sniping had continued while Colin had conducted his rough surgery, but no one else had been hurt. The oxen and other livestock cooped within the circle had not been so fortunate. They almost filled the area between the wagons and the Indians had only to drop their arrows within that area to be sure of hitting some kind of target. The lowing of the injured beasts, most of whom suffered superficial wounds, merged with the crying of the children and the deep curses of men who, staring into the darkness, could see no sign of their enemy.

'Douse the fire,' ordered Colin. He snatched up a water bucket and threw it on to the central fire. 'Quick, douse the fire.' He turned to Sam. 'Tell the men to keep extra sharp lookout. With the fire gone the Indians will be sneaking closer.'

'Should we have kept the fire?'

'The animals are getting wild. If they collect a few more injuries they'll break loose and smash a hole through the wagons. The fire was scaring them and the smell of blood frightened them.'

Colin stared up towards the sky. 'Maybe we'd better drive the oxen out of the circle.'

'If we do that the Indians will slaughter them,' said Sam. 'Then what'll we do?'

'Have men watch the beasts. If they show signs of stampeding then drive them into the open. Tie them to the lead poles and tie them firm.' He swore as a trail of fire arced through the air. 'Fire arrows! Stand by the buckets!'

His warning was none too soon. The fire arrows, each wrapped in burning, grease-soaked rag, were dropping onto the canvas covers of the wagons and only prompt action saved a disastrous fire. Men tore at the arrows with their bare hands, dashed water on burning canvas and stamped other, poorly aimed shafts into the dirt. The tiny flames licking from the shafts threw a fitful light over the scene, reflecting from the faces of men and showing their figures against the darkness.

The Indians were not slow to take

advantage of such targets.

'Three dead and five injured.' Sam, his face burned and his hands blackened, reported to Colin. 'Three dead,' he repeated bitterly. 'And we ain't fired a shot yet.'

'No sense in making holes in the air.' Colin stared again at the sky. 'Until we can see the Indians we'll have to wait it out. Come dawn we may be able to have a crack at them.'

'Maybe.' Sam wasn't optimistic. 'But it looks as if they'll burn us out before then.'

He was wrong. The clouds which hid the stars had brought rain and long before dawn a sudden downpour rid the wagoners of the threat of fire. They welcomed it, holding up their faces so as to feel it on their cheeks and, as the fire arrows ceased, their spirits rose.

'Reckon it'll send the devils back home, Colin?' Sam had recovered his spirits. 'We ain't had no arrows for 'most an hour now.'

'They won't be afraid of a little rain.'

Colin stared grimly about the camp. He had ordered a small fire to be lit in order to boil water for the wounded and to give them light by which to calm the restless animals. Heaps of brushwood cut down the light and a sheet of tin protected the tiny blaze from the rain. In the dim light men and women moved as they tried to mend the burned covers of their wagons in order to protect their contents from the rain. From one wagon came the groans of the wounded. Sam tilted his head towards them.

'You going to doctor them, Colin?'

'Butcher them, you mean.' Colin shrugged at the other's expression. 'Hell, Sam, I sure ain't no doctor. I learned a thing or two during the war but that was all.'

'You're the best doctor we got,' insisted Sam. 'I would never have thought of that trick of pouring whiskey on the wounds. Seems to me that it would hurt too much.'

'Better a little more pain now than

have the wound begin to rot later.'
Colin didn't want to talk about it.

'Someone's got to help them.' Sam
glanced at the young man. 'I'll help if
you want me to.'

'Thanks.' Colin scowled, then, suddenly, took a drink of whiskey from the
jug Sam carried. The raw spirit burned
his throat but it also warmed his
stomach and dissolved some of the
tiredness from his limbs. 'Well, let's get
it over with.'

It was near dawn when Colin and
Sam descended from the wagon, both
red with blood up to the elbows. Sam
was shaken and Colin looked white
beneath his tan. He washed himself in a
bucket of water and then, his hands
clean, took a long drink from the
almost empty jug. Behind him a couple
of women tended the wounded, wrap-
ping them in blankets and placing
pillows under their heads. A third
carried blood-stained rags to the fire
and threw them on the blaze.

'One thing I'm sure of,' said Colin.

'I'm never going to become a doctor.'
He shivered a little both from memory
and the pre-dawn chill. 'I guess that I
just don't like hurting people.'

'You did a good job.' Sam dried
himself on the tail of his shirt. 'I've seen
old Doc Henderson back home make
more mess and take more time than
you did. The way you cut out that
arrow from young Tom was a sight to
see.'

'Maybe.'

'I tell you it was. Most times we used
to call in the horse doctor but one time
my Uncle Joe fell over a harrow and cut
himself up real bad. Pa washed him and
we put some herbs on the cuts but they
wouldn't stop bleeding. So we called in
Doc Henderson. I had to ride ten miles
and promise him a sucking pig before
he would come. Well, after he'd got
through sewing up poor old Joe he was
fitten to be taken for an Indian, he was
that red. I . . .'

'Indians aren't red,' said Colin
sharply.

'What's that you say?' Sam screwed up his eyes.

'They aren't red, that's what I said.'

'Sure, I know that. I was only using a figure of speech. Something wrong, Colin?'

'No.' Colin shook his head. 'Sorry, I was thinking of something else.' He sighed as he stared towards the east. 'Sure wish it was dawn.'

'Sure wish that Julia would come riding back with the soldiers,' said Sam. 'But I guess we'll have to wait for that.' He sighed. 'But I'll be glad when the sun comes up, I'm getting hungry.' He sniffed at the air. 'It won't be long to sunup now. Maybe we can eat then.'

But when dawn broke the horizon the Indians attacked.

10

They came like a wind, a sudden, terrible rush of mounted figures, their painted faces and bodies giving them the appearance of grotesque fiends straight from the floor of Hell. They fired as they charged, arrows and bullets tearing the air and, as they raced against the little circle of wagons, the screaming war whoop of the Sioux echoed across the plain.

'Colin!' Sam snatched up his rifle and flung himself down under a wagon. 'Colin!'

Colin did not move. He stood just between two wagons and stared at the advancing Indians. He felt numb, stunned, stricken with something he could not understand. Before him the Indians seemed to swell, to grow huge, an array of painted faces, streaming feathers, wild-eyed ponies and the glint of steel-tipped lances, barbed arrow heads and the more modern barrels of repeating rifles.

They looked like devils, inhuman in their paint and beadwork, their screaming war whoop shattering the air as a prelude to the humming arrows, the bark of rifles and the thud of their horses' hooves.

For Colin time had dissolved, slipped back to a night long ago when the stench of burning flesh had filled the air and he had crouched, trembling with fear and horror. He re-lived through that same fear and horror and, deep within him, he wanted to run, to hide, to bury himself deep in the earth, to get away from the painted devils who were charging towards him.

'Colin!' Sam stared towards the young man, then at the charging Indians. He swore, not understanding why Colin should just stand there, doing nothing, saying nothing, just staring with eyes which seemed to hold all the terror that ever was.

'Get set,' he yelled to the wagoners. If Colin could not give orders then Sam knew that he had to fill the breach. 'Aim careful and squeeze gentle. Fire on the word.' He waited, the smooth stock of his Winchester tight under his chin, his finger curved around the trigger. An arrow slashed towards him and stood quivering scant inches from his head. A woman screamed as a rifle bullet tore into her side.

'Fire!'

Smoke plumed from the circle of wagons and lead whined towards the Indians. Ponies crashed to the ground and shrieking Indians toppled from their mounts. In a moment the thundering charge had become a blood-reeking shambles but even then the Indians did not stop. Those towards the rear swung their mounts past their stricken comrades, screamed their war whoop again and, suddenly, were among the wagons.

Lithe bodies leapt from their horses and, tomahawk in hand, rushed towards the few defenders. Two of them raced for a gap between the wagons where a tall young man stood staring at them with horrified eyes. The first Indian screamed as he flung himself forward at the hated white man, his tomahawk lifting high as he readied himself for a blow which would split the skull.

Then Colin came to life.

There is a limit to fear. No matter how paralysed a man may become there is a point at which he must struggle for life. Colin had reached that point. He had lived through his youthful terror and, suddenly, it had burned itself out. Instead something else took its place so that now he no longer felt fear towards the Indians. He felt hate.

His hands fell to his holsters and his Colts were roaring even as they cleared leather. The first Indian spun backwards with a bullet between the eyes. The second screamed in agony as lead slammed into his stomach, then the young man sprang onto the lead pole of the wagon and was pouring lead into the mass of surging bodies rushing towards him.

As usual in battle Colin felt a strange detachment. He seemed to be standing aside watching himself as he thumbed his hammers and fired again and again into the whooping Indians. His guns empty, he jumped back, snatching up a rifle and working the lever until it, too, was empty. Then he sprang forward again, the rifle clubbed in his hands and his detachment vanished in the surge of hand to hand combat. He swung the rifle again and again, sending it crashing down on painted faces, knocking aside reaching lances as if they were straws and automatically dodging the tomahawks which swept towards him. He fought like a man insane with hate and, as he fought, his eyes blurred so that he felt nothing but the mounting thrill of dealing death to a hated enemy.

'Colin!'

He snarled and swung and fought against something which held him.

'Colin, you crazy fool!' Something

dashed into his face and he coughed as water filled his mouth. 'Colin!'

It was Sam. He stood holding the young man, an empty water bucket by his side. He was wounded, a thick stream of red running down over one cheek. Colin blinked, shook his head and drew a deep breath. Abruptly he was calm again.

'What is it?'

'You had me scared.' Sam stared hard at the young man then released his grip. 'You was fighting like crazy. Didn't you know we'd beaten them off?'

'No.' Colin stared at the rifle he still grasped in his bands. Its stock was shattered, the barrel thick with blood and the grey-white matter of human brain. His hands and arms were covered with blood, his jacket and shirt torn from his body. Around him, lying where they had fallen, a dozen Indians gave mute testimony to his savage onslaught.

Colin dropped the ruined rifle and crossed to a water bucket. He dipped his head, washed his arms and torso and discovered, to his mild surprise, that he carried a half dozen minor cuts and slashes. He felt for his guns and re-loaded them, then, picking up a rifle he loaded that, too. His weapons ready he stared about the camp.

The Indians had been so near to complete success that it was hard to understand why they had retreated. The space between the wagons was a shambles. Dead animals littered the ground and those that were not dead had broken free and escaped onto the prairie. Men, both white and Indians, lay in pools of their own blood. Wounded wagoners cried for water and two of the wagons had been overrun by the Indians. They had contained women and children but the attackers had not discriminated. Young and old, men, women and children, all had been slashed and stabbed to death. Some of them had even been scalped and the cries of women as they recognised their slaughtered men-folk and youngsters added to the hideousness of the scene.

'God!' Sam was very pale. 'They done near wiped us out.' His eyes ran over the dead and dying. 'God,' he said again, and was suddenly very sick. Colin waited until the farmer had recovered himself.

'Let's get tidied up,' he ordered. 'Clear the wagons and gather up all the weapons. Check to see who is fit to use a gun. Those that can't can reload for those that can.'

He jumped on to a wagon as Sam moved among the survivors and stared at the Indians circling the camp. They rode low on the necks of their horses, keeping a continuous though scanty fire directed towards the camp. Arrows and bullets whined and hummed across the prairie, thudding into the ground, whining through the canvas tops of the wagons or hitting the woodwork with dull impact. Something burned a path down Colin's side and he looked down to see blood well from the bullet graze. Automatically he took cover, keeping his eye turned towards the Indians.

His fear had quite gone and only hate remained. To him the Sioux were little more than blood-crazed devils, hardly human in their terrible ferocity. They were set on killing every man, woman and child in the wagon train and only the guns of the wagoners could keep them away. But where the Indians numbered hundreds the wagoners were few. Colin jumped down to join Sam.

'How many can we muster?'

'Not enough.' Sam still looked pale from his inner sickness. 'Eight men are fit to handle the guns and as many women reckon they can shoot. Some of the youngsters are able to load.'

'Is that all?'

'Yes.'

'And the wounded?'

'I've counted in the wounded. The rest are either dead or can't handle or load a gun.' The farmer dabbed at the wound on his scalp. 'Things are bad, Colin.'

'They could be worse.'

'You reckon so?' Sam shrugged. 'I doubt it. The next charge will wipe us out if it's anything like the last one.' He scowled towards the Indians. 'What's keeping them back, Colin? Why don't they ride in and get it over with?'

'In a hurry to die, Sam?'

'I'm getting tired of waiting.'

'They'll come soon enough.' Colin ducked as an arrow hissed past his head. 'Make sure that everyone is under cover and has spare rifles to hand.' He looked around the camp. 'The trouble is this circle is too big now. We can't hold every part of it. I'd like to make a strong point, build a barricade so that we can concentrate our fire.' He scowled at the wagons. 'Reckon we could move them into a closer circle?'

'We could try.' Sam cleared his throat, then stiffened as a man yelled a warning.

'Here they come!'

'Hold your fire!' Colin snatched up his rifle and leapt to his post. 'Wait for my signal.'

'What's the plan, Colin?' Sam clutched at the young man's arm.

'No plan.' Colin was terse. 'We fight as best as we can for as long as we can. Keep the Indians away from the wagons. Keep firing at all costs. Unless we can beat them back with a hail of lead they'll overrun us.'

He took careful aim as the yelling Indians came closer, breaking their circle and swooping towards the wagons. Their charge was concentrated on the point where Colin stood and he waited, finger tense on the trigger, as they came closer and closer.

It was not like the first time. Then there had been fear and disorganization as the Indians advanced. That fear had turned into hate and a grim resolve to fight to the last man and the last bullet. Now the wagoners, what was left of them, aimed and fired at the advancing shapes, triggering their weapons until the hammers clicked on empty chambers, then tossing aside the useless weapons and snatching others. Behind them the women and children re-loaded, thrusting cartridges into chambers, forcing themselves not to look at the enemy.

Colin, firing with cold precision, found time to be thankful that weapons had improved since his first encounter with the Indians. Had Zeke carried a cartridge belt things may have been different. But it was only at the outbreak of war that the cap and ball pistols had been replaced with the cartridge type. Now he could fire and fire and fire and know that he could re-load with a minimum of time.

The breaking of their first charge had unsettled the Indians. The murderous fire which met their second unsettled them still more. They swung back into a circle, bending low over their horses and sending a stream of bullets and arrows into the huddle of wagons. Many Indians died, but the wagoners suffered also.

Colin knew, with bleak certainty, that defeat was only a matter of time.

'Four men dead and five women,'

reported Sam grimly. 'Three wounded. Hell, Colin, we ain't got a chance.'

'We'll have to close the circle,' decided the young man. 'We can't hold all the wagons. Get the men and come and help me.'

He ran to the lightest of the wagons, rapping swift orders.

'Strip off the tailboards. Get the water barrels, flour sacks, anything and everything you can think of to build a barricade. Get three wagons moved closer together and stack the stuff around them. Get the children and wounded inside. Hurry!'

His plan was simple but carrying it out was something else. The wagons were heavy and the Indians kept up their fire. Sweating, panting, struggling with the dead weight of the supplies, the men moved and carried the material for a barricade over to the designated point. Tugging and grunting they moved two wagons against a third to make a rough triangle.

'That's it.' Colin dashed the back of

his hand above his eyes to clear them of sweat. 'Now stack the flour and tailboards against the wheels.'

'You reckon it'll do?' A small, wiry man asked the question, then, before Colin could answer, he grunted as if he had been struck. His eyes glazed and he toppled to land face down on the ground, the feathered shaft of a war arrow standing up between his shoulders. Colin swore, snatched a pistol from his belt and fired at the warrior who had ridden in close to the wagons to shoot the killing arrow. Twice Colin thumbed the hammer and twice the weapon roared its defiance. The first shot missed, the second did not. The warrior screamed, throwing up his arms and falling from his mount.

'Nice shooting,' said Sam. He looked worriedly at the deserted wagons. 'What if the Indians get among them wagons, Colin? They'll be under cover the same as us.'

'I know it.' Colin thrust two fresh cartridges into his pistol, snapped closed the side gate and spun the chamber before slipping it into its holster. 'We'll have to move them away.' He looked at Sam and the others. 'It's the only thing to do, now hurry!'

Once again they threw themselves against the stubborn wagons, trying with their limited strength to do what four spans of oxen normally did. They gripped the wheels and swore as their feet slipped on the grass. They cursed as invisible death whipped around them, then redoubled their efforts at the thought of what would happen should the Indians capture them alive. Slowly the wagons moved away from the crude barricade.

'Wish we had some dynamite,' panted Colin. 'I reckon we could give them Indians a surprise.'

'We ain't go no dynamite,' said Sam. 'But I had a keg of blasting powder in my wagon. You want it?'

'Where is it?' Colin glanced again at the circling Indians. They were curious, wondering what the white men were doing and had slackened their fire. Colin felt contempt for their military prowess, any sub-commander would have known that an attack now would carry the field. The Indians, unused to discipline and acting only as a collection of individuals, had no one to direct their attack. So they rode and stared and wondered what the white eyes were doing.

The blasting powder was large-grain gunpowder and mostly used to split rocks and uproot tree stumps on virgin land. Dynamite was better but more expensive and many miners and most farmers used blasting powder. Unlike dynamite it needed no detonator, but was, of course, much less powerful.

'Here she is,' said Sam. He set down the small, heavy keg. 'What you aim to do, Colin?'

'Set a trap.' Colin took out his knife and stabbed a small hole in the top of the keg. He tilted it and a thin stream of coarse black grains fell to the ground. From his cartridge belt he took a shell, bit out the bullet and thrust the brass case into the hole. It fitted reasonably tightly. Lifting the keg Colin placed it in the nearest wagon so that the primed head was pointed towards the barricade.

'Now let's get to our positions,' he ordered. Hold your fire until we need it; we're getting low on ammunition.'

He hesitated while the others ran for cover, then rummaged among the contents of the wagons. A broken lamp yielded some oil and he scattered it over the dry timbers around the powder keg. Then he covered the keg with clothes taken from chests, mirrors, iron cooking pots, anything and everything which would both hide the keg and attract the Indians.

Then, running and bending low, he raced towards safety.

He made it just in time, the Indians, their patience exhausted, re-opened their fire. Colin squatted down behind a flour sack, hearing the thud of lead as it buried itself in the white powder, and stared towards the little group of wagons about twenty yards away. His eyes were good and he could see the little round cap of the cartridge case winking at him in the light. Carefully he took aim at the bright point, satisfied himself that he could hit it, then lowered his rifle.

'All right,' he said. 'Now we wait.'

'Wait for what, Colin?'

'Wait for the Indians to investigate. They know we've abandoned those wagons and, from them, they can command this position. It's certain that they'll make an attempt to take them. They will, we can't stop them, but when they get settled we'll give them something to think about.' He glanced up at the sun, now hanging directly above. 'Issue water and food, Sam. Let everyone check his weapons and try and relax. Shoot if you have to but don't shoot to keep the Indians away from those wagons.'

'Anything else we can do, Colin?' Sam looked up from where he sat by the water barrel.

'You can relax,' said Colin. 'Or you can pray. But there's nothing to do now but wait.'

So they waited while the sun blazed down from above and the Indians crept closer.

11

It was hard that waiting. There was nothing to do but sit in behind the barricade and watch, to listen to the moans of the wounded, the fretful cries of the children, too numbed by horror to fully realize their position. Mary, Sam's wife, miraculously uninjured, soothed the children as best she could and stared with longing eyes towards the distant horizon.

'She's thinking of Julia,' said Sam, softly to Colin. 'She don't say much but I can tell what's on her mind.' He sighed. 'Think she got through?'

'Maybe.'

'There were two men with her,' said Sam. 'She was well armed and well mounted. She had a chance, didn't she Colin?'

'She had a chance.'

'A good chance?' Sam wanted reassurance.

'She probably made it.' Colin glanced up at the sun. 'If the map was right and nothing went wrong she should be on the way back now. The fort ain't so far for horsemen to travel.' Colin shrugged, dismissing the thought. 'She'll be back when she can. Quit worrying about it, Sam.'

'Wish she'd hurry,' said Sam. He took a mouthful of water, held it against his teeth then slowly swallowed. 'Wish we was well out of this.'

'Wishing won't get you anywhere,' said Colin sharply. 'You've got to rely on yourself and the guns you carry.' He paused, squinting through the loophole he had made in the barricade. He gave a sound, half-amusement, half-contempt. 'They've fallen for it. The Indians are making for the wagons!'

They came like lithe brown shadows against the dry, sun-scorched grass. They had ridden cautiously up to the far side of the clustered wagons and, finding them empty, gained courage. Others joined the initial party, then more, all eager for the loot to be found within the high-walled bodies and beneath the canvas tops. Yells and the sound of breaking echoed from the wagons. A man, more foolish than brave, lifted his head and stared towards them.

'Down!' Colin spun, his face full of anger. 'Get down!'

'What?' The man stared at the young man. 'You mean . . . '

He screamed, a high-pitched thin sound, and his hands clawed desperately at the arrow imbedded in his throat. He opened his mouth and blood gushed forth as if from a fountain. He reared, kicking in his final agony, then collapsed lifeless on the ground.

From the wagons the triumphant yells of the Indians merged with the reports of rifles and the deep thrum of bowstrings. Arrows and bullets thudded into the barricade or whined overhead.

'Down!' Colin hugged his sack of flour. 'Keep down!'

'What if they rush us, Colin?' Sam

had realized the danger. 'Unless we can see they'll be on us before we know it.'

'We must chance that.' Colin squinted cautiously through his loophole, feeling the satisfaction as he saw the tiny circle of brass reflected in the sun. 'They are twenty yards away and those Indians are good shots. If we try to trade fire with them we'll be wiped out after the first volley. If they charge we'll have to rear up and let them have it with everything we've got, but not until we have to.' He twisted his head. 'Keep a sharp watch on the other sides, we don't want the Indians to try a sneak attack.'

'When you going to blow the powder, Colin?'

'Soon.' The young man stared towards the wagons. I want to get a full load while I'm at it.'

Over in the wagons the yelling and frenzy had increased. Colin took a deep breath, raised his rifle and gave last instructions.

'Keep down and cover your faces.

Have water handy and, as soon as you hear the explosion, douse any fires. Those who can be spared from water duty rear up as soon as things have stopped falling and pour lead into everything moving you can see. Ready now, take cover!'

Slowly Colin aligned the rifle. Before him the head of the keg with its shining cartridge case seemed to draw his eyes. He tensed his finger then flinched as lead tore the flour sack within inches of his face, filling his eyes with the fine white powder. Before him, kneeling almost on the keg, an Indian pointed his Winchester for a second shot.

Colin hesitated for a split second. He could kill the Indian but, if he did, the man might fall forward and cover the primed keg of blasting powder. On the other hand his next shot might well find the loophole and drive into Colin's brain. It was a time for instant decision and Colin, forcing himself to ignore the Indian, squeezed the trigger of his rifle and immediately threw himself face down on the ground.

Beneath him the prairie seemed to rock beneath the impact of a mighty blow. The air was full of a terrible roaring and a vast cloud of smoke rose from where the wagons had stood. From that smoke, screaming, blinded, torn and injured by the explosion and the splintered wood, Indians staggered and fell to the ground. Fire, licking at the sun-dried woodwork, added to the horror of the scene.

'Water!' Colin slapped at flames springing about him carried by specks of burning powder and chips of flaming wood. 'Douse these fires!'

He snatched the Colts from his belt and fired into the staggering warriors. Smoke swirled all around him and the leaping tongues of flame were dimmed by the reeking cloud. From that cloud came a terrible screaming as Indians, broken and crushed by the explosion, felt the flesh sear from their bodies as the flames of the burning wagons lapped around them.

'Keep firing!' Colin dropped his empty guns and snatched others, his thumbs rolling the hammers as he swung them level. 'Keep firing!'

Around him the barricade blazed with flame, the smoke of the guns adding to the smoke of the explosion. Indians, blinded and dazed by the terrible thing which had happened to them, staggered and fell as hot lead smashed into their bodies. Stunned and terrified by the inexplicable, dying where they stood from the guns of the defenders, they wavered and then fled.

'We've won!' Sam wiped his red-rimmed eyes, coughing from the reeking smoke. 'We've beaten them.'

'No.' Colin thumbed fresh cartridges from his belt and reloaded his pistols. He slipped them into their holsters, reloaded two more and stuck them handy in his belt. He checked his rifle and stared towards the flaming ruins of the wagons.

'They're running,' said Sam. 'Look at them go!'

'Some are running,' corrected Colin. 'But the rest weren't touched by the explosion. And there are still more than enough of them to overrun us and wipe us out.'

He didn't like to say that, to wipe the look of hope, from Sam's face, but Colin was a man who lived with facts and had no time for useless hope. Julia may or may not have got through. She may or may not be on the way back with relief but it didn't matter. Nothing mattered but the Indians circling them again and the hot sun above and the harsh, sickly smell of blood filling the warm afternoon air. That and the reek from the burning wagons, the old, familiar reek of flame seared flesh and even though this time it was Indian flesh that was burning and not the bodies of his folks it made no difference.

Colin shook his head, conscious of a sudden weakness and from the pain in his stomach, realized that he had not eaten for too long. He wasn't hungry but he forced himself to fill his mouth with corn bread and wash it down with tepid water. A man needed food inside of him if he had to fight. A man could face death better if he wasn't hungry and death had been very close that day. It had been closer than at any time in his life before, except, perhaps, when he had touched off the bomb and jumped from the bridge. That had been close but then he'd only had one enemy and once it was over he could relax. Now he had a hundred enemies and death was only a matter of time.

'Colin!' Sam stared at the young man and shook his arm. 'You all right?'

'I'm all right.'

'You sure don't look it.' The farmer thinned his lips. 'You look like a man who's just been kicked on the head by a horse, or maybe a man hurt inside some way. You sure that you're all right?'

'Damn you, yes!' Colin swallowed and wiped the back of his hand across his forehead. What could this farmer know of the bitter pain of memory?

'I wish we had some whiskey,' said Sam. 'I sure could do with a swig of it right now.' He shook his head. 'Mary tells me it's all gone.'

'Is she all right?'

'Seems to be. She's been doing some real hard praying by the look of her. I can always tell when she's been praying hard, her eyes turn kinda red.'

'She's been doing some hard fighting too.'

'I know.' Sam stared over Colin's shoulder and his face tensed. 'This is it,' he said softly. 'God! Look at them come!'

Over the plain the Indians had broken their circle and now, in one compact body, were racing towards the tiny band of defenders.

'Hold your fire!' Colin flung himself into position. 'Aim at the horses and fire on the word. Steady! Fire!'

Winchesters ripped the warm air with lances of fire and horses screamed as lead smashed into their bodies, sending them kicking and rolling on the red-stained grass. Above the screaming war whoops of the Indians, the whinnying of the horses, and the thunder of hoofs, Colin's voice sounded with calm assurance.

'Fire again! Get their horses. Save the pistols for close quarters. Blast them, boys! Let them have it!'

For an agonizing moment it seemed as if the hail of load from the barricade would smash the Indians away from the defenders then, with the shocking abruptness of an earthquake, the defenders were fighting hand to hand for their very lives.

Colts flamed and flamed again as the roaring pistols sent lead into lithe brown bodies. Men swore and screamed as lance and knife, tomahawk and rifle swung and slashed at head and bodies. Colin, his hands working as with a life of their own, thumbed the hammers of his guns, pulling trigger until the hammers clicked on empty chambers, then discarding the

213

guns for the spare ones in his belt.

For a while everything was cursing confusion, the reek of blood and gunsmoke heavy in the air, the scent of Indian smell and sweat, the flashing lights from polished blades and discharging guns. Then, abruptly, it was over and the Indians, screaming and brandishing their weapons, raced towards the horizon bearing away their dead and wounded.

'They've gone!' Sam, his left arm hanging limp and his clothes ripped and stained with blood, stared after the retreating Indians as if he saw the answer to a prayer. 'They've gone,' he said again. 'It's a miracle.'

'Maybe you could call it that.' Colin felt very tired. He had been awake and fighting for as long as he could remember. His wounds burned and his eyes were red from powder-smoke and fatigue. He pointed towards the north. 'See that smoke?'

'I see it.' Sam squinted his eyes as he stared at the distant column rising towards the sky.

'That's a smoke signal. The Indians must have seen it and decided on one last charge before pulling out.'

'But why?' Sam was puzzled. 'Hell, we was as good as dead. What would make them pull out like that?'

'There's only one obvious answer.' Colin sagged against the barricade. 'They left because they were scared to stay. The only reason they could have been scared is because a stronger force is heading in this direction.' He paused. 'A force of white men.'

'Julia!' Sam almost shouted the word. 'She must have got through.'

'That's right.' Colin smiled at the farmer. 'Tell Mary that her prayers are mighty powerful. The smoke from the explosion may have guided them, of course, but it's still a miracle.'

'Yes,' said Sam, then sobered as his eyes travelled over the shattered remnants of the wagon party. He walked over to his wife, still miraculously unharmed, but she was the only one.

All the rest bore wounds, some minor, some so serious that it was obvious they would not live. Mary, heedless now of saving, was issuing water to all who needed it.

'It's bad,' he said as he rejoined Colin. 'Miracle or not it's bad.'

'Can a miracle ever be bad?'

'I don't know.' Sam shook his head, like Colin he was feeling the reaction of the fighting now that it was over. 'All I know is that most of the folks I talked into coming out here with me are dead. Mary's alive, and Mrs Shaw and her children. Langthorne's wife and youngsters are dead. Abe Hyam's alive, though he'll probably lose an arm and his wife will recover. A couple of the youngsters are untouched and three more have minor wounds.' He beat his clenched fist into the palm of his other hand. 'But all the rest are dead, Colin. Why did they have to die?'

Colin didn't answer.

'They came looking for a new life,' said Sam bitterly. 'They sold up and collected what they could and followed me into the Nations. I talked them into coming. I promised them free land, good land, a place where they could settle. But what have we left? A handful, no more.'

'That's enough.'

'Enough for what?'

'Enough to settle down and start that new life you were talking about.' Colin stared seriously at the farmer. 'You can't conquer a wilderness without losses, Sam. You can't fight a war without people getting killed, yes and women and children too. And this is war, Sam, as much a war as the one which ruined the South. White men have got to take over this land, they've got to do it if for no other reason than that they can make better use of it than the Indians can. So they have to fight for it, but, is that bad? Do men value what they get without trouble? One thing is certain, once you settle down here you'll never move. You'll have bought the land the hardest way there is. You'll have paid for it in blood and the death of your friends. That's the only real way to pay for land, Sam, you have to fight and die for it. When you do that then it's truly yours.'

'Maybe you're right, Colin.' Sam stared about him then lifted his eyes to where twinkling points of light had suddenly appeared over the horizon and were moving swiftly towards the wagoners. They moved fast did those points of light and he knew them for the flash of spurs, the gleam of buckles and other metallic pieces of the uniformed cavalry which had come to the rescue.

Ahead of them, racing forward as fast as her horse could travel, a tall, red-haired figure was clearly recognisable. Sam glanced at the young man at his side.

'And you, Colin? Will you stay with us?'

'I don't know,' said Colin. 'I just don't know.'

'Julia would like it if you could,' said Sam.

'Maybe!' Colin didn't answer and Sam was too wise to press the point. 'I may stay, I may not. I just don't know.'

Sam knew. He had seen the way Julia had looked at the young man and he knew what would happen. Colin would stay. He would marry Julia and together they would help conquer this new, rich land. He would do it because, even though he hadn't admitted it, even to himself, he was in love with the tall, red-haired girl, but he would do it for a deeper reason than that. He would do it because it was the only thing he really wanted to do.

He would do it because he was a true son of the West.

THE END

We do hope that you have enjoyed reading this large print book.

Did you know that all of our titles are available for purchase?

We publish a wide range of high quality large print books including:
Romances, Mysteries, Classics
General Fiction
Non Fiction and Westerns

Special interest titles available in large print are:
The Little Oxford Dictionary
Music Book, Song Book
Hymn Book, Service Book

Also available from us courtesy of Oxford University Press:
Young Readers' Dictionary
(large print edition)
Young Readers' Thesaurus
(large print edition)

For further information or a free brochure, please contact us at:
Ulverscroft Large Print Books Ltd.,
The Green, Bradgate Road, Anstey,
Leicester, LE7 7FU, England.
Tel: (00 44) **0116 236 4325**
Fax: (00 44) **0116 234 0205**

THE GALLOWS GANG

I. J. Parnham

After escaping the gallows eight condemned men, led by Javier Rodriguez, blaze a trail of destruction, leaving swinging bodies as a reminder of the fate they'd avoided. Four men set out to bring them to justice: prison guards Shackleton Frost and Marshal Kurt McLynn; Nathaniel McBain, a man wrongly condemned himself and under suspicion from Frost and McLynn, and the enigmatic man known as The Preacher. Can this feuding, mismatched group end the Gallows Gang's reign of terror?

LEFT-HAND GUN

Walt Masterton

Grasping landowner Morgan Fetterman hires a professional gunman to get rid of Jemima Penrose from her ranch in the mountains of Arizona. However, his mistake is to choose Luke Horn for the job, because he dislikes what he hears about Fetterman. Then Horn, despite a disabling wound in his right arm, assists in getting rustlers brought to justice. But amid the plotting and gunplay, can Horn, Jemima and old guy Fed Sauermann bring Fetterman's plans tumbling down?

THE LIBERATORS

Brett Landry

When General Grant Westerly of the defeated Confederate Army arrives home he finds his parents murdered and his house a ruin. Only Joseph remains, to tell him about the terrible slaughter that had occurred at the hands of five deserters from the Union forces. When Grant and Joseph pursue the vengeance trail, heading south and then north through Indian country, hardship and danger are their constant companions. Only their determination and fighting skills can bring the murderers to justice.

QUICK ON THE DRAW

Alan Holmes

Detained for a crime he had not committed, Glenister McCreedie is released on parole from prison. However, later that night, Glenister finds himself with a dead prison guard on his hands, and he flees to the railway construction town of Keedie. There his past catches up with him and he's forced to break his parole as he confronts brutal mule skinners and fights cattle thieves and train robbers.

RULE OF THE GUN

Bryan Shaw

On the run from the law, Vince M'Cloud and his gang decided to take over the sleepy little town of Arrow's Flight and use it as their hideout. After killing the sheriff, M'Cloud instituted a tyrannical reign of gun law, holding the town under siege. Anger simmered amongst the populace, and plans of revenge were afoot. But it was the appearance of the mysterious outlaw Abe Fletcher that really threatened to turn events around . . .

FIRES OF VENGEANCE

John Russell Fearn

When Clem Dawlish and Amos Grant discover a valuable oil field near the town of Carterville, they plan to eliminate the ranchers and homesteaders in order to stake their claim. They create a phantom to head a gang of outlaws and destroy the ranchers. The scheme works and Dawlish becomes a power in Carterville. But another phantom arises: one who would avenge all who had died at Dawlish's orders. Now the law of the gun — and justice — would surely prevail.